MEN WHO WALK WITH DRAGONS

MEN WHO WALK WITH DRAGONS

JAKE DEKKER

NICETIGER

NICETIGER
Printed and published electronically in the United States by NiceTiger Publishing

"Your Own Song" © by Jim Quigley
reproduced by permission

"The Velveteen Rabbit" by Margery William
Public Domain

Cover art © by Sunniva Myster reproduced by permission

Cover layout by Scott Fleming

ISBN: 978-1-937777-99-9

Library of Congress Cataloging-in-Publication Data available.

*To my father Peter and
his ancestors*

*To my son Casey and
his descendants*

*And to my nephews Peter,
Blaine and Jake*

Contents

There comes a time
When even the master's music
Can't compare to your own song,
Your own song is the one
That will carry you home.
        — Jim Quigley

CHAPTER ONE

FINDING YOUR DRAGON

AUTHORS NOTE

Although this book is written to help men learn to walk with dragons most, if not all of it, applies to all genders.

"People who deny the existence of dragons are often eaten by dragons. From within."
— *Ursula K. LeGuin*

What does it mean for men to walk with dragons? Doesn't everyone know that dragons aren't real? They don't come tearing out of the sky breathing fire on anyone's home or neighborhood, nor do they visibly attack people who harm others. Almost all we know about dragons comes from stories, movies, books, art and myths.

Dragons are mythical creatures, but does that mean they never existed? The veracity of myth is one of our great mysteries. Did Noah really bring two of every animal on an ark before God flooded the world and killed every other living being? Was there a leader who united his kingdom and changed the relationship of monarch to knight by creating a round table? And if Arthur did exist, did Merlin use magic to guide and serve him?

Some describe myth as that which is always true but never was. A dragon is a creature of magic. It is as at home in mystery as a dolphin is in the ocean. The natural habitat of the dragon is not familiar to our conscious mind. Dragons live in the lands of legend, stories, magic and myth. Their natural home is a land of quests, heroes, courage, betrayals, victory and mistakes.

In the land of the dragon, the brave, noble hero always succeeds, even if his success involves his death. In the world of dragons, a hero must die to his old life to live his destiny.

Everyone has a destiny. A potential. A calling from life itself to heroically live and discover the journey we were uniquely born to take. One way to think of this is to imagine each of our lives as a mysterious seed, and the goal of life is to develop and grow from that seed into whatever wonderful, one-of-a-kind creation nature intended us to be.

Many of us know little about our potential. We forget that we can develop and grow into a person far beyond our conscious imagining.

"To walk with a dragon" includes remembering that we

are here for more than material well-being, pursuing the illusion of security or endlessly distracting ourselves with romance, media, food and the internet.

Somewhere in every person's consciousness is an awareness that discovering and becoming who we really are is our birthright and our greatest commitment to ourselves. No one has the right to take that away from us. While society, culture, bullies and others try to steal our birthright, we often discover that no one has taken as much from us as we have taken from ourselves.

Usually the biggest threat to learning to walk with a dragon and discovering who we really are comes from within. We believe we aren't good enough, or "I'm a loser," or "I don't have anything to offer," and if that false belief is allowed to persist, we generally descend into depression, resignation, anxiety and fear.

Fortunately, it isn't true. Each one of us carries a unique piece of the human tapestry, without which all of humanity is incomplete. There is almost nothing we can do that is more important than encouraging ourselves and one another to discover who we really are and live the life we are born to live.

All beings walk in at least two worlds. There is "this one", the world where we were conceived and born, where we progressed from infancy to childhood and beyond and where we wake up every day. It is what most of us call "the real world."

We also walk in another world. Sometimes we glimpse

and remember that world in our dreams, or feel it when our spine tingles from a sudden inspiration, a "coincidence," or a feeling of déjà vu.

It is the world beyond the two great mysteries of birth and death. Most of us have seen it, but we don't always recognize it. In the same way that our ears can't hear every high or low musical tone, and our eyes can't see every color created in the sky, our primary physical senses can't perceive everything around us.

There is a part of every one's being that knows we belong to more than this world. Our birthright includes more than we usually remember or what we see, hear, taste, touch and smell. It is in that dimly recalled, difficult to see place, that dragons live.

In this "real" world, men are usually judged and perceived by what they accomplish and do. Men tend to judge each other by what they materially provide in this world, not who they are inside, or their fidelity to their calling.

In the other world, what is important is becoming who we are intended to be. To walk with dragons, we must let go of our focus on outcomes and be brave, courageous and relentless in pursuit of our calling regardless of our prospects for success.

How do we discover our calling and recognize who we really are? We must learn the difference between the external things that beckon to us, and the wisdom that calls us from inside our deepest selves.

Many of us don't hear destiny's call, or if we do hear it, we don't answer when it knocks on our door and calls us to a larger life. Too often our destiny rots like a basket of fresh fruit forgotten at our front door. There comes a time in the growth and development of all of us when we must choose between the siren's call to seek security in this world, or the dragon's call to become a hero.

The price of heeding the dragon's call is to face the challenges, fears, and dangers that always accompany any worthy quest. The price of surrendering to the siren's seduction is apathy, disappointment and an uneasy sense that life is meaningless and our most important opportunities were missed.

Men who walk with dragons answer their callings, strive to live their destiny and don't shirk from their quest. Courage, duty, loyalty, compassion and wisdom are some of the qualities that define them. It isn't easy, and the journey includes loneliness, suffering, fear and discouragement. But it also includes triumph, excitement and the incomparable joy that comes from doing what is right for us.

Walking with dragons requires a fierce commitment to forge a relationship with a wild beast. It will test you, for there is no such thing as a tame dragon.

To walk with a dragon means to befriend and integrate the wild, unseen, fantastical and magical parts of your being with that part of you who you already know. It means risking the ultimate sacrifice, with the certainty that something within us must die to allow something new to emerge.

When we walk with dragons, we don't need to be afraid. We are discovering and following our own path. Walking with dragons carries the promise that everything we need for our journey is right beside us.

The stories in this book will help you walk with dragons. The best stories are constructed from more than the words that create them. They can be magic. There is wisdom that comes from the ageless messages in each of these tales. Each story has layers of meaning. While some possibility of how each story may help you is described, the deepest messages in each story are found individually as you read, contemplate, imagine and dream. The wisdom in stories isn't found by learning what others think about them. It is found in discovering what a story means to you.

CHAPTER TWO

DESTINY

The most important journey any of us take is to discover our destiny, our calling, and to learn who we really are. The idea that something within us informs, nudges, affects, guides, teaches and supports us seems common to all cultures and people.

Proving that each of us has unconscious resources is as simple as recognizing that our heart regularly beats, yet our conscious mind doesn't regulate it. When we see a young child in distress, we almost universally respond with an impulse to help. There is something deeper than our consciousness that tells our heart to physically beat and also tells us to care for those who are in urgent need.

In addition to our legacy and obligation to serve the common good, we each have a unique mission or role in life that we are most suited to perform. When we discover our purpose and integrate it into our daily life, walking with dragons comes as naturally as waking up in daylight.

To discover who we really are takes effort. It usually doesn't come easily. For most of us, there are clues in our childhood and earliest memories. The experiences and feelings that inspired us when we were young can often act as guides. Stories, movies and myths that inspired us as boys often point the way to our destiny as men.

Whether we exulted at the faith of Luke Skywalker as he put aside the viewer to make his final run on the Deathstar, Robin Hood as he stole from the rich and gave to the poor, Batman as he protected Gotham City, Simba as he avenged the death of his father, Tip as he willingly became Ozma of Oz, Mowgli as he learned to live in harmony with the animals in the jungle, Harry Potter as he grew past the grief of the death of his parents and fought injustice and evil, or Edmund as he succumbed to the temptations of the White Witch in Narnia but eventually forswore her…in these stories and many more, the seeds of destiny are sown.

One of the most well-known stories of a young man finding his destiny is the story of Arthur and the sword in the stone. There are many versions of this story, and experts have spent years of research trying to identify the most accurate account.

The version I know best isn't faithful to scholars. It's the story I heard when I was a child, told for a boy's understanding.

THE SWORD IN THE STONE

Once upon a time, when England was a wild and rugged place, there lived a king named Uther. There were some who didn't recognize Uther as their king, but after many years he united the squabbling dukes, earls, barons and counts, defeated all the invaders and was accepted as the one and true king.

Uther found a wife and made her his queen. But when their son was born, the great magician, Merlin, came to Uther and said, "I am sorry your majesty, but your reign is cursed. There is nothing I can do to save you, but I can save your son."

"But everything is fine," Uther protested. "Nothing is wrong here!"

Merlin sadly shook his head. "Things aren't what they appear, your majesty. In less than a year you will be betrayed and killed, and your son will die too unless you give him to my protection."

Because of the faith Uther had in Merlin, he gave his son to Merlin's safekeeping. "Watch him well," Uther warned. "For the fate of all England rests with this child."

Merlin left the castle with the prince and hid him where no one, not even those who now cared for him, knew he was the crown prince. As Merlin foretold, within a year Uther was betrayed and killed. Because there was no heir apparent, a dark time came over the land.

The invaders that Uther had vanquished returned, and they attacked the nobles, peasants and villagers. The dukes, earls, barons and counts resumed their battles. Robbers attacked travelers on the highways, and fear engulfed rich and poor alike.

Sixteen years after King Uther's death, the archbishop

of Canterbury summoned Merlin. Although the magical forces wielded by Merlin were heresy to the church, the unrest in England was so terrible that the archbishop was willing to consider anything to restore peace.

"The dark times are everywhere, Merlin," the archbishop complained. "Since the death of King Uther we have lost all hope of peace, and I fear that our country is doomed. If only Uther had left an heir to the throne."

Merlin's eyes twinkled. "I have good news, your grace. Uther had an heir, and his son is alive. Before his death, Uther gave him to my keeping. He is a young man now, but not even he knows who he really is. The only way I could protect him was to keep the knowledge of who he is to myself."

"How can we restore him to the throne?" the archbishop gasped.

"If you grant me dispensation to use magic and prove that Uther's son is the rightful heir, I will create an event that leaves no doubt that Uther's son is the one true king."

The archbishop slowly nodded. "Under normal circumstances I could never allow your magic, but these are desperate times, and I fear that England will be gone forever if I don't allow this. So yes, I grant you permission to use your magic to return Uther's son to the throne."

"Thank you, your grace."

"What is the boy's name?" The archbishop asked.

"His name is Arthur."

On the next Sunday morning a giant block of stone

with an anvil mounted on top appeared in the brick courtyard in front of the archbishop's cathedral. Plunged into the anvil was a flawless sword. The blade was crafted from the finest steel, and the golden hilt was decorated with exquisite jewels. Carved in the stone was this message:

> *Whosoever Pulleth This Sword*
> *From This Stone And Anvil Is*
> *The Trueborn King of England*

Noblemen, dukes, earls, barons, counts, merchants, pages, squires, villagers and even a few stable boys placed their hands around the hilt and tried to draw the sword. But not even the strongest blacksmith nor the most powerful knight could move the sword in the stone. It stood impervious to all.

After a few weeks, the knights and noblemen grumbled, "This sword can't be pulled by any man." And indeed, after a few months passed the efforts to draw the sword from the stone diminished, as did the hope that a king would return to the throne.

The archbishop sent a message to Merlin advising that no one could draw the sword from the stone. "The people are losing interest in it, Merlin," the archbishop wrote. "Hope is fading and I don't know what to do."

"Hold a tournament," Merlin replied. "Invite every major and minor noble from across the kingdom to compete, and allow anyone who thinks he is worthy to attempt to draw the sword from the stone."

Invitations from the archbishop swept across the land.

A great tournament to see who had the most prowess and strength was announced, and all the nobles across England made preparations to attend.

Far away from the archbishop's cathedral lived a gentle, kind knight named Sir Ector. Although Sir Ector was too old to compete himself, he had two sons. The older was strong and handsome. He had been only recently knighted and given the title of Sir Kay. The younger son, Arthur, looked about 17, but Sir Ector wasn't sure of his exact age as he had adopted Arthur as an infant.

"Father," Sir Kay shouted. "There's to be a tournament for all the knights in England! We must go!" He shoved the proclamation into his father's hand.

"Yes, I see," Sir Ector mused, "and there is to be a contest to see if anyone may draw the sword from the stone and be crowned King of England."

"We must go, Father," Sir Kay insisted. "It will take a few days to get there, and I don't want to miss anything…" Sir Kay paused. "But Father, I am a new knight and don't have a squire to serve me."

"I am sure your younger brother would serve as your squire if you ask him."

"Arthur! Father! Arthur doesn't know anything about being a squire. He spends too much time in the woods and not enough time jousting. Only last week I saw him set a rabbit free that was caught in a trap!"

"Your brother has a good soul," Sir Ector said mildly.

"He doesn't like to kill animals for sport unless we are hungry, and fortunately we have plenty to eat."

"But, Father, must I ask Arthur?"

"Yes. That is my command. It will be good for the two of you to serve as knight and squire and the three of us shall attend the tourney together."

Yes, Father," Sir Kay said, for he was a dutiful son and a loyal knight.

Sir Kay asked Arthur to be his squire. Arthur happily agreed. To Sir Kay's surprise, Arthur did an excellent job of polishing his armor, packing his traveling clothes and making sure his brother had all he needed to turn in a fine performance at the tournament.

Despite the unrest, the highways were safe as many knights, dukes, earls, barons and counts made their way to the great contest. The festive mood continued when they arrived at the tournament, where Sir Kay registered to compete and Sir Ector greeted old friends. Arthur continued to carefully mind his brother's belongings, and Sir Kay decided Arthur wasn't really such a bad squire.

The tournament grounds were the largest anyone had ever seen. Tall stands for the nobles were erected with fine views of the jousting and battle fields. Merchants erected booths to sell food, drink and colorful banners to wave and encourage their favorite knights. Horses, knights in armor, colorful tents and crowds of people created a feeling of excitement that Arthur had never experienced.

On the first day, Sir Kay participated in the jousting. Arthur did a fine job of helping his brother buckle his armor, attach his helmet, mount his horse, hold his shield and secure his lance. After the first two skirmishes, Sir Kay was still upright and barely wounded.

"See, Arthur?" he proudly proclaimed, "I have only one scratch, near my breastplate. That wasn't so hard." Arthur smiled at his brother's pride. "Of course, tomorrow will be harder," Sir Kay added. "We have to fight with swords."

The next morning dawned gray and dismal. Light rain had fallen in the night, the tourney field was muddy, and the tent awnings were wet with dew.

Arthur could see his brother was nervous. Although Sir Kay was a fine horseman, he wasn't as competent a swordsman. Arthur had spent several hours polishing his brother's sword, battle ax and mace. He wanted to make sure all of Sir Kay's implements were in perfect shape.

The brothers left their tents early so Sir Kay could practice. Arthur gathered the weapons and placed them in a sling on his horse. When they arrived at the competition grounds, they dismounted. "Let's start with my sword, Arthur. That's the weapon I need most today."

Arthur removed the weapons from the horse, but when he went to retrieve the sword, it wasn't there! His heart leaped in his throat. "I'm so sorry, Sir Kay," he stammered. "I must have forgotten your sword!"

"Forgotten my sword!" Sir Kay shouted. "How could you be so stupid? That's the most important thing!"

"Don't worry, I'll hurry back and get it. I'll be right back." Without waiting for a reply, Arthur galloped his horse back to their tents, but the sword wasn't there. *What will I do?* He wondered. *I only had this one duty and my brother will blame me forever. Maybe the sword fell when we were riding,* he thought. Arthur mounted his horse and retraced their path, but no sword was there.

Arthur was desperate. He had a little money, but only enough for food. He couldn't buy a sword. For a moment, he thought of stealing a sword. But as soon as that idea occurred to him, he banished it. He was Sir Ector's son, and his father had taught him to be honest and true.

Hopeless, and not knowing what else to do, he rode his horse to the large cathedral. The stained-glass colors washed over him as he knelt in prayer and asked that he might be able to fulfill his duty. When his prayer ended, he left the cathedral, still not knowing what to do.

As he approached his horse, he saw a bright light so intense that it forced him to blink. Turning, he saw the sun had broken through the clouds and bright rays reflected from a gleaming sword set in an anvil and stone. The steel appeared the finest he had ever seen, and the hilt was cast of gold.

This must be the answer to my prayer, he thought. *I'm sure this sword wouldn't have appeared to me unless it was to help me get a sword for my brother.* Murmuring a quick prayer of thanks and a promise to return it, Arthur approached the sword in the stone.

As he put his hand around the golden hilt and pulled, the sword immediately broke free. Without hesitating, Arthur rode to his brother. As he approached, he could see the anger in Sir Kay's eyes.

"It about time you got here," Sir Kay growled. "Now hand me my sword."

"I am sorry, brother," Arthur apologized. "I couldn't find your sword. I checked the tents and our trail, but it wasn't there. I didn't know what to do, so I went to the cathedral and prayed. As I was leaving, this sword gleamed as if in answer to my prayer. It's a really nice sword, and when you are done using it, I'll put it back where I found it."

Sir Kay's eyes grew large as Arthur handed him the sword. He immediately recognized it as the sword in the stone. For a moment, he wondered what it would be like to claim it as his own and become the King of England.

But Sir Ector had raised two fine sons, and Sir Kay was also true. He gently told his squire and brother, "Come, Arthur. We must go see father immediately."

"But what about your practice?" Arthur protested.

"It means nothing now." The brother's rode to their father and when Sir Kay extended the sword to Sir Ector the older man gasped in confusion.

"Kay...but how did you, how could you be..."

"It wasn't me, Father," Sir Kay interrupted. "It was Arthur."

"Tell me what happened, Arthur," Sir Ector quietly instructed his son. Arthur recounted the story of how he acquired the sword. "Come with me, my sons." And Sir Ector led them to the cathedral where the stone and anvil looked empty without the sword.

"Arthur, can you please put the sword back in the stone?" his father asked. Arthur placed the sword into the anvil, and it effortlessly glided back in place. Sir Ector looked at Sir Kay, "Go ahead, Kay," his father implored. But despite all his efforts, Sir Kay couldn't budge the sword at all.

"But, Kay," Arthur said, "Surely you can move the sword. We both know you are stronger than I am."

"Arthur," Sir Ector asked, "can you please draw the sword from the stone?" Arthur placed his hand on the sword and swiftly pulled it over his head.

"Now I know who you really are," his father said. And to the surprise of both Sir Kay and Arthur, the old knight knelt before his younger son.

"Father," Arthur pleaded, "what are you doing? Surely you know who I am. I am your son."

"Maybe once, and always in my heart but, my dear boy, you have a destiny that is beyond mine. Can you read the letters carved into the stone?" Arthur turned and read the inscription.

Whosoever Pulleth This Sword
From This Stone And Anvil Is
The Trueborn King of England

"The trueborn King of England," Arthur said confused, "but how can I be?"

From across the deserted courtyard a hooded man approached. "Hello, Merlin," Sir Ector said. "I guess I shouldn't be surprised to see you here today."

Merlin nodded in greeting. "Sir Ector, you have done a great service to England. Can you please tell Arthur how he came to be your son?" So, Sir Ector explained to Arthur and Kay that when Arthur was an infant, Merlin had come to him and asked him to raise Arthur as his own child, but to never tell anyone that Arthur wasn't his own son.

"Arthur," Merlin said, "you are the blood son of King Uther and the hope of England. Sir Ector has kept you safe all these years and now you are called to unite England as her true and rightful king."

"But what about my father and brother?" Arthur asked.

"Sir Kay can still be your brother, in heart if not in name, and Sir Ector will always be a father to you," Merlin replied.

"Must I do this? Can't I return home to the life I know and the people I love?"

"No, Arthur," his father gently interjected. "You know how dangerous the countryside is and how men battle, rob and hurt each other. England needs you. This is your destiny. It is what you are born to do. Sir Kay and I will always help and support you, but if you give any credence to me as the man who has strived his best to be your father, I implore you to accept your birthright as our king."

"You have always guided me true, Father." Arthur said. "So I will do as you tell me, but you and Sir Kay are always my family and though I will serve England, my heart will always be with both of you too."

Tears welled up in Sir Kay and Sir Ector's eyes as they came forward and embraced the young man they loved whom they now recognized as their liege and king.

Merlin nodded. "So shall it be. Now return the sword to the stone so we may show the people that you are their newfound rightful king."

The next day the archbishop and Merlin announced that the time had come for all present to try to draw the sword from the stone. Once again, all the dukes, earls, barons and counts, the victors of the tournament and many knights tried. But none could move the sword at all.

Finally, the archbishop called loudly, "Are there any others who would seek to draw the sword from the stone?"

"Yes, your grace," Sir Kay said. "I would like to try." Sir Kay grabbed the sword, but he could not move it. "Your grace," Sir Kay asked, "I would like my squire, Arthur, to try. May he have your leave to attempt to draw the sword from the stone?" The archbishop nodded, and Arthur, dressed in a simple red tunic stepped to the sword in the stone.

Unlike all the others, Arthur did not immediately attempt to draw the sword. Instead, he looked at each man, woman and child present. The crowd grew quiet as Arthur looked at each in turn. Everyone in the courtyard felt something was different. Finally, Arthur closed his eyes, bowed his head, and murmured a prayer as a crown of sunlight formed a nimbus around him. As his prayer ended, Arthur opened his eyes and with a look of love, grace and nobility, he drew the sword that was his birthright and effortlessly raised it over his head.

"All hail Arthur, the true King of England," the archbishop commanded.

"All hail Arthur, the true King of England," the crowd chanted in reply. Cheers began to rise and a feeling of joy and hope greater than anyone present had ever felt swept through the crowd.

Arthur smiled at his subjects as he raised his sword in greeting to all. And so began the greatest age of knights that the world has ever known as Arthur, now King Arthur, began his reign.

*
* *

Trying to find our destiny is a little like trying to find our best friends. Sometimes we search and feel alone, or we think we found them and then are betrayed. Often our closest friends don't appear where we were expecting them. We may find them because we were assigned a school locker together, a dorm room in college or a seat beside each other on a bus.

Part of the way to find your destiny and discover who you really are is to keep looking. Usually we discover it over time. The important thing is to never quit seeking.

Most of society's sanctioned distractions are a soporific. They lull us into an apathetic lethargy that inhibits us from seeking to discover our destiny and who we really are.

As we get older, the pressures of providing for ourselves and our partners, wives, husbands, parents and children grow. Society tells us that a man is defined by what he can produce and accomplish. Net worth is valued more than integrity. Personality is valued more than principles. Looking good on the outside is more important than feeling good on the inside.

But all of this is a lie. It's made up. It isn't true. What defines us is not how we appear to the world, it's how we feel and think about ourselves.

One way to know we are truly discovering our destiny is when we quit trying to constantly conform to who our parents, teachers, friends and family tell us who we should be, and instead, learn to be guided by our inner voice.

Walking with dragons requires discovering who we really are and then acting on it. It means living our destiny no matter what society says about how we should be, act, feel, think or do. It means learning to trust ourselves and our inner wisdom. It means learning that when men walk with dragons they are never alone because everywhere they go they are accompanied by the wild, untamed, magical dragon alongside them.

The wounds the man felt as a boy, the doubts and uncertainty of being a teenager, and the Sisyphean task of becoming a mature adult are healed, reconciled and transmuted as we learn to walk with dragons.

Chapter Three

WHO YOU REALLY ARE

While we may think we know who we really are, often we really don't. Self-realization is a lifelong process that leads us closer and closer to understanding who we really are.

Although the statement, "we don't know what we don't know," may seem obvious, it is the starting point for self-discovery. Discovering who we really are usually comes slowly over time.

In *The Velveteen Rabbit,* it took a long time for the rabbit to start to understand who he really was as he became "Real."

"Real isn't how you are made", said the Skin Horse [to the rabbit]. "It's a thing that happens to you. When a child loves you for a long time, not just to play with, but really loves you, then you become Real."

"Does it hurt?" asked the Rabbit.

"Sometimes," said the Skin Horse, for he was always truthful. "When you are Real, you don't mind being hurt."

"Does it happen all at once like being wound up," he asked, "or bit by bit?"

"It doesn't happen all at once. It takes a long time. That's why it doesn't happen to people who break easily or have sharp edges, or have to be carefully kept. Generally, by the time you are Real, most of your hair has been loved off and your eyes drop out and you get loose in the joints, and very shabby. But these things don't matter at all, because once you are Real, you can't be ugly, except to people who don't understand."

In the same way that the rabbit took a long journey to becoming "Real," each of us takes a lifelong journey to finding out who we really are.

Heroes hate bullies. Dragons do too. One of the greatest gifts of discovering who we really are is that the words, taunts and cruelty of others lose much or all of their potency over us.

When we know who we are, the clarity of our understanding creates a field of protection. Once we have a sense of who we really are, we can't be hurt in the same ways.

When I was young, I wasn't good at any sports. I threw a ball awkwardly, I ran poorly, and I was afraid to try anything I thought I looked stupid doing. I was terrified of people laughing, teasing or making fun of me.

When other kids called me "gay" or a "loser," it tore me apart. I didn't have the mental, emotional or spiritual strength to respond. Instead, I felt a deep, searing pain. My feelings were much more intense than they needed to be, because I didn't have the ability as a child or teenager to handle challenging feelings the way I have learned to now.

Ironically, I was attracted to boys, and as a young adult accepted that I was gay. But at the time, my confused feelings of physical attractions only deepened the pain I felt.

I wish I had possessed the courage back then to tell the bullies, "Yeah, I am gay. So what? I'd never be attracted to an a-hole like you!" When we claim our identity, and embrace who we really are, we find a strength and foundation that allows us to go through situations and challenges that we never thought we could handle.

Each of us is a piece of the divine tapestry of life without which our human family is incomplete. In the land of dragons, all of us are divine royalty with missions to fulfill.

In that land, we learn that none of us are home until all of us are home. Each of us is an indispensable piece of the whole, and we need each other. We must learn to be kind to each other and tolerant of different points of view and beliefs. We need to love each other or none of us are complete.

Feeling different, awkward and unworthy can lead to depression, anxiety and suicide. The truth is that it is our differences, strangeness and eccentricities that are usually our greatest gifts. The irony is that what we often loathed and tried to hide about ourselves can prove to be our greatest gifts. This idea is demonstrated beautifully in the story of a young duck who couldn't fit in and eventually discovered who he really was.

THE UGLY DUCKLING

It was beautiful in the country. It was summer, and the wheat fields were golden, the oats were green, and down among the meadows the hay was stacked. In the midst of the sunshine stood an old manor house with a deep moat around it. From the walls of the manor down to the water's edge great leaves waved in the breeze.

Under the leaves, a mother duck sat on her nest, hatching her ducklings. She was becoming weary. Sitting is a dull business and scarcely anyone came to see her. The other ducks preferred swimming in the moat to waddling out and visiting her.

At last the eggshells began to crack, and one after another the ducklings poked out their heads and emerged from their shells.

Soon they waddled out together to look at the green world under the leaves.

"How green and large the world is," said the young ducklings, for they had much more room now than they had enjoyed in their shells.

"Oh, the world is much bigger than this," their mother kindly said. "It extends on and on, beyond what the eye can see and further than the bravest duck can fly. I do hope you are all hatched, No, not quite all. The big egg still lies here," she said as she turned and looked back at her nest.

How much longer is this going to take? She wondered as she settled back on her nest.

"Well, how goes it?" asked an old hen duck who came to pay her a visit.

"It's taking a long time with this one egg," said the mother duck on the nest. "It won't crack, but look at the others. They are the cutest little ducklings I've ever seen. They look exactly like their father, the wretch! He hasn't come to see me at all."

"Let's have a look at that large egg that won't crack," the old duck said. "It's an odd egg," she said skeptically. "I had an egg like that once. It turned out to be a turkey egg! Maybe you have a turkey egg. It's awfully large."

"No. I don't think it's a turkey egg. It's just a little different than the others. I'm sure it will be all right," she said

"Suit yourself," said the old duck as she waddled away.

A few days later, the large egg cracked and a young bird tumbled out. He wasn't anything like his brothers and sisters. He was large, awkward and gangly and appeared to be all beak and legs. His feathers were peculiar, and his eyes didn't look right.

His mother looked at him and thought, *Oh my, he's a frightfully big and ugly duckling. He must be a mutant!*

Still, he was her child and she wanted to help him. The next day the mother duck led her whole family, including the newly hatched large duckling, down to the moat. One after another the ducklings plunged in. The water went over their heads, but they came up in a flash and floated perfectly. Their legs worked automatically, and even the big duckling was soon swimming in the moat.

"Now that you can swim, I'll lead you out into the world and introduce you to the barnyard. But keep close to me!"

They did as she told them, and the other ducks and barnyard animals looked on and told her how well her children swam and how beautiful they were as they passed by. "Wait. Is that one yours?" someone asked.

"What is wrong with that one?" another called.

"What an ugly-looking bird that is! He can't live with us!" a proper old duck protested. As soon as the words were spoken, a strong duck charged up and bit and pecked the young duckling's neck.

"Let him alone," his mother said. "He isn't doing any harm."

"Not yet," said the duck who bit him, "but he's big and strange and he's not welcome here."

"What nice-looking children you have, Mother," said an old mother duck. "They are all pretty except that one. It's a pity you can't hatch him again."

"Well, I think he will be quite strong, and I'm sure he will amount to something," his mother defended him.

Soon her young ducklings felt quite at home. All except the poor duckling who looked so ugly. He was hissed at and pecked and pushed about and made fun of by the other ducks. Even the chickens teased him. His brothers and sisters shunned him. They wanted to be accepted by the other young ducklings, and it wasn't respectable to have anything to do with their odd brother.

Soon the poor duckling was so ashamed that he took to hiding under the eaves or porch whenever he could. He constantly wondered why he was so ugly and what would ever become of him.

Things went from bad to worse. The ducks nipped him, the hens pecked him, and the girl who fed them kicked him with her foot.

His mother tried to defend him from the ducks and hens, but there were too many. They hissed and pecked and hissed and pecked until he barely had any feathers and his body was covered with wounds.

No matter how much she defended him, the duckling wouldn't stand up for himself. He simply withdrew and tried to hide, which was impossible because of his awkward size.

One day, in a fit of exasperation, his mother said, "What is wrong with you? Why don't you just leave here?" So he did.

He hopped and he flew and he hopped and he flew and sadness and despair washed over him because no one loved him and he had no place to go.

That evening he reached a great marsh where some wild pheasants lived. He lay there all night alone, weary, and feeling hopeless

In the morning some young pheasants came to have a look at their new companion. "What sort of creature are you?" they asked. "You are awfully ugly," they told him.

"I know," he said.

"Well, you're really young, but we are going to head over to the other county. We heard there are some young pheasants over there and they are single. Do you want to come with us?"

He shook his head no.

"Suit yourself," they said. As the pheasants flew away, the loud sound of gunshots filled the air and the pheasants fell to the ground dead. All around him birds were shot and killed. The young ducking lay perfectly still, while bullets splattered through the reeds. It was late in the day before things became quiet again, and even then, the poor duckling didn't dare move. He waited several hours before he ventured to look about him, and then he hopped and flew away from that killing marsh as fast as he could go.

Late in the evening he came to a little shack in the woods. An old woman lived there with her cat and hen. Seeing the young duckling she decided to let him in. "I have a hen that lays eggs," she said, "maybe this bird will lay eggs too." But of course he couldn't lay any eggs.

"So, what good are you?" asked the cat. "You don't like mice, and you don't catch anything."

"I don't know." said the duckling.

"And you don't lay eggs?" asked the chicken.

"No, I've never laid an egg."

"There is something wrong with you," said the chicken. The cat hissed at him in agreement, and they taunted and tortured the poor duckling until a few days later he flew away from their house.

Winter was coming on. The leaves in the forest had fallen and the skies looked cold. The duckling had no place to go, there was no one in the world that wanted him. He wandered from marsh to field to lake. His heart was full of despair, and he didn't know what would become of him.

One evening, just as the sun was setting in splendor, a great flock of large, handsome birds flew overhead. The duckling had never seen birds so beautiful. They were dazzling white, with long graceful necks. They uttered a strange cry as they flew, and from inside the young duckling emerged a loud, strange sound he had never made before. It was if he knew their language and wanted to reply. They circled around. One tipped a wing at him, and they flew off into the sunset. It was the most beautiful thing he had ever seen, and his heart was momentarily filled with hope. But soon they were gone.

The winter had grown so bitterly cold that the duckling had to swim to-and-fro in the water to keep the ice from freezing over. But each night the hole in which he swam kept getting smaller and smaller.

One night it froze so hard that the duckling had to paddle continuously to keep the crackling ice from closing in upon him. At last he fell asleep and was frozen fast in the ice.

Early the next morning, as the duckling was stuck in the ice, he saw a man approaching him bearing a large axe. *So this is how it ends*, the duckling thought. *At least I saw those beautiful birds.*

As the man approached, the steel of his axe gleamed in the icy, morning sun. The young duckling stretched out his neck, closed his eyes and waited for the final blow. Part of him wanted to die. He wanted the pain to end. But as he submitted to his fate, he felt sad that this was the end of his life. It seemed there should be more to life than being teased, wounded and banished from every place he tried to make a home. He remembered the beautiful birds and how they filled his heart with hope, and he wished he had lived a life that knew their grace and beauty.

The axe fell hard and he was still alive! It fell again and the young duckling was able to move! The man wasn't trying to kill him. He was freeing him from the ice.

As soon as he was free, the man carried the young duckling home to his family. There the duckling revived, but when the man's children tried to play with him, he thought they meant to hurt him. Terrified, he fluttered into a milk pail, splashing the room with milk. The mother shrieked and threw up her hands as he flew into the flour barrel. "Look," she said, "he battered himself. I guess we better fry him up and eat him, as that must be what he wants." The children laughed and shouted, but the window was open, and the duckling escaped. He flew a short distance to a field where he landed in the newly fallen snow, where he collapsed in a daze.

It was a hard and cruel winter. The young duckling believed he had tried every possibility, but there was no refuge for him. Eventually, he found a small place to hide, and there he stayed through the winter. Isolated from the world, he emerged only enough to scavenge food and then hide again. Sometimes he thought of the beautiful birds. It was the only hope he knew. He didn't know what would become of him, or what was his purpose, but he did know enough to survive the cold winter.

As the weather warmed and early spring came, the young ducking realized that his wings were longer, his feathers had grown, and despite the cold winter he was stronger. He no longer had to hop and fly, his wings were strong. One morning he flew away from his hiding place, determined to find a lake or a marsh or a pond where he could stay. As he was flying, he saw a beautiful small lake. It was surrounded by trees, and the water was clean and pure. There were reeds along the edges to nap in and plenty of places to forage or to hide.

He touched down on the lake, landing like an angel. He swam by himself, enjoying his newfound strength. An odd feeling came over him and he looked to the sky. In the distance he could see some birds flying toward him. As they came into view, he realized the most beautiful birds he had ever seen had returned, and his heart leaped with hope and joy. Tears fell as he cried at their beauty. They uttered the same odd call he had heard months before, and this time he responded with the same call in his own voice.

The birds changed course and flew toward him and landed on the water where they glided gracefully. They formed a beautiful white circle as they slowly swam around him.

"Oh," the young duckling cried, "Please take me with you. I have no place to go, and no one who loves me."

"What's the matter brother?" They asked. "Don't you recognize us?"

"No. I only know you are beautiful and that I want to be with you."

"We are no more beautiful than you. Haven't you looked at your reflection and seen who you really are?"

And the young ducking realized that because he was always told he was ugly and he was always teased and pecked and hurt that he had been afraid to truly see himself. But there in that moment, surrounded and supported by the love and grace of the beautiful birds, he felt the courage to truly look at himself and see who he really was.

As he stared intently into the water, he realized his beauty, and he knew he was home at last. These were his people. This was his tribe. He had always belonged, but he didn't know it until now.

So he swam from the center and joined the circle with his new family and friends. Together, the graceful, beautiful swans flew up from the lake. The young duckling, who now knew he was really a swan, was filled with hope as he flew with his brothers and sisters toward the promise of freedom that he'd always hoped for in his heart.

*
* *

All of us can be each other's angels. In some ways, life is very simple. We can choose to bedevil each other and become each other's demons, or we can choose to love each other and become each other's angels.

Although there are many paths for a man who walks with dragons, we must strive to become angels to each other on every path we choose, or our journey is doomed. Dragons won't walk with or aid men who bully, taunt, harm or are cruel to others.

By the time we are ready to live our calling, we must be committed to serving others, to acting as an angel to those in need. We must understand that walking with dragons always includes becoming an angel every time an opportunity to do that presents itself.

It is inevitable that opportunities to help others will arise, the trick is to have sufficient intuition, discernment, wisdom and integrity to recognize and answer the call wisely, every time the call to be an angel is sounded.

Fortunately, we are human and making mistakes is part of our heritage. The universe and dragons seem forgiving of our errors, as long as we acknowledge them, change them and learn from them.

Another challenge that inevitably arises is that when we successfully answer the call to help others, we receive praise, approbation and thanks. We run the risk of forgetting that when we act as angels to others, the power, strength and abilities we show are not our own. We are channels.

Power and the desire to influence can become temptations. The lure to become a predator, tyrant or despot

traps many. It's as if when we mature and develop suffi-
ciently to act as an angel to others, we simultaneously at-
tract the attention of a force that would have us enslave
others rather than help them. The ability to be a channel
for good carries the potential to be a force for chaos.

One of the true tests of any man who walks with dragons is our ability to exercise integrity in our moments of
choice. Problems and temptations will come. Our integrity will be tested. There are many distractions that will
tempt us to leave the path of our quest, including riches,
unhealthy attractions, rage, hubris, jealousy, envy and
pride. To stay true to our destiny, we must know, embrace
and learn to love who we really are.

When the swans say, "What's the matter brother?...
Don't you recognize us?" and tell the younger bird that he
is as beautiful, graceful and angelic as all the swans surrounding him, the younger bird sees for the first time who
he really is. He finally discovers the truth that he is everything he admired in others.

The journey the young bird had to take to come to
this realization was long, arduous and filled with physical,
mental and emotional pain. In addition to being hungry
and cold, he was teased, reviled, pecked to near death and
abandoned by his "mother."

The young bird didn't know how to respond to these
terrible assaults on his body and soul, so he withdrew, isolated and lost hope.

When he reached the end of his ability to take care of

himself, he saw the hunter coming to kill him as he was frozen in the ice. Rather than protest his death, he surrendered. He had come to the end of all he could do to survive, and he resigned himself to whatever fate the universe or destiny had for him.

As he slowly lowered his head and extended his neck on the ice so the hunter could smite off his head, part of him was relieved that the terrible pain he felt would finally end. As the axe struck, his world changed. He realized the hunter wasn't there to kill him after all!

Sometimes the things we think will kill us are what will set us free, and sometimes the things we think are our salvation turn out to be our greatest peril.

The young bird learned a valuable lesson. He discovered that when we go as far as we can go, when all our excuses and fantasies are stripped away, there is something there to support us. For him, it was the hunter whose axe rescued rather than killed him.

Why did the hunter do that? Why did he free the young bird instead of kill him? Something inspired him to free the bird from the ice. Perhaps it was witnessing the humility of the young bird bowing his neck in surrender, or maybe he was called by a power greater than himself to free the bird. He didn't have to do it. No one would have protested if he killed the bird or had left him to die from the frozen trap. But he didn't. He freed him.

It is answering those calls, hearing and acting on those

impulses, that we make the transformation from the ordinary to the angelic. When we learn who we really are, we gain the ability to be of unique and powerful service to others. We become ready to hear the calls that are uniquely ours, that we were born into this world to answer.

CHAPTER FOUR

INTUITION

No man who walks with dragons is naïve, so one of the first steps to walking with dragons is to move from the innocent state of the child to maturity.

While the pain, joy and experiences of life guarantee that much of a child's innocence and naivete are eventually lost, most men fail to recognize and claim their birthright of intuition and wisdom as they lose their childhood innocence. All men have a resource to help guide their maturation from child to boy to young man and beyond.

It is the gift of inner knowing, the whispering of the soul, what society sometimes calls a "woman's intuition." And that description, probably more than anything else, is likely why so many boys and men fail to claim it. In the culture of boys becoming men, few sacrileges are greater than "acting like a girl," or being a "sissy."

Some of the worst insults boys can hurl to each other are: "You throw like a girl!" or "Boys don't cry." To the young boy, almost universally unprepared for the power in these accusations and unable to integrate the resources within him that society associates with the feminine, his only recourse is to deny, avoid, try to prove they aren't true or suppress them. Otherwise, he risks being taunted and teased by whatever cruel words others use to ostracize and hurt him.

It's painful enough when these insults come from other boys, but too often the words and subsequent pain come from fathers, brothers, uncles, teachers, coaches and grandfathers. When that happens, the family or cultural ground of security and love the boy thought was firm shifts, and a wound of feeling unwanted, unloved or unworthy that can persist for a lifetime is formed.

It is difficult to learn to walk with a dragon when a man is stuck in his wounds. Often the feelings and stories about the wound are greater than the damage itself. Dragons require a lot of inner space, and it's hard to give them room when a man's inner life is dominated by the stories of his wounds.

One of the first steps to walking with dragons is to reclaim or create a connection to inner knowing and reclaim the wise guidance of the soul. In the story of Aladdin, a young, immature boy discovers his inner wisdom through a combination of personal effort and good fortune, and in doing so he eventually becomes aligned with his path of destiny.

ALADDIN AND THE MAGIC LAMP

Once upon a time, there lived a poor, good-hearted boy named Aladdin. He and his widowed mother struggled to make ends meet. Aladdin wanted to help provide his mother a good home, but he wasn't skilled at any craft and he preferred playing in the streets with his friends to working. He and his mother were often hungry, and as Aladdin grew older he paid less and less attention to his mother's advice.

One day in the market, Aladdin met a man who said he was his father's best friend. Aladdin's memories of his father were dim, and he was excited to talk to someone besides his mother who could tell him stories about his dad.

The stranger said that Aladdin's father was brave and wise, but there were secrets that Aladdin's mother didn't know.

"Now that you are becoming a young man," the stranger told Aladdin, "I need to tell you of the treasure your father left you."

Aladdin swelled with pride. He always secretly believed his father had done something to help him and his mother, so he followed the stranger across the desert to a large outcrop of stone.

The stranger paused and said, "Your inheritance is beneath these rocks. But you must do exactly as I say! Your father left traps to protect your treasure from thieves."

"I will!" Aladdin said excitedly. He couldn't wait to see the treasure his father had left him.

"First, I will move a stone with magic, and you will see a dark hole. You must climb down on a rope."

Aladdin felt uncomfortable. He didn't like the dark. "Are there spiders?" he asked.

"No, nothing lives there. The drop is a small distance. Once you land, you must follow the stairs down to a large chamber. There you must carefully cross the chamber, taking care not to touch anything! You will see great treasures and jewels, but you must not touch any of it or you will be killed. If you stay on the stone path, you will be safe. At the end of the path you will see an old lamp nestled in an alcove high on the stone wall. Climb the wall, grab the lamp and bring it to me."

"How do I get the treasure my father left me?" Aladdin asked.

"After you bring me the lamp I will cast a spell so you can get your treasure."

"I'm going to share it all with you!" Aladdin said, for he was generous.

"No, no," protested the stranger. "I promised your father that all of this is for you and your mother. Your happiness is reward enough for me."

Aladdin hugged the stranger and said, "I'm ready to go. Even though I am afraid of the dark, I will be brave."

"What's the most important thing?" the stranger asked.

"Don't touch anything but the lamp," Aladdin answered.

The stranger cast a spell, and a large rock rolled on its side revealing a hole just wide enough for Aladdin to slide underground. The stranger pulled a long rope from his pack, secured one end to the rock and tossed the coil down the opening. It made a small thud as it landed.

Aladdin grabbed the rope and quickly reached the

stone landing. It was dark, and the cavern floor felt hard under Aladdin's feet. He lit a candle and cautiously made his way down the cold, stone steps. His candle reflected treasures and jewels. His heart leaped with excitement but, remembering the stranger's warning, he stayed on the path.

At the end of the path, nestled high on a stone wall was an old brass lamp. *I don't know why with all these treasures he wants that ugly old lamp*, Aladdin thought. He set his candle in the wall, climbed up to the alcove and placed the lamp under his arm.

He carefully made his way back on the path, trying not to look too often at the jewels and treasures that enthralled him. "I'll be back for you soon," he whispered as he approached the stairs.

An odd feeling came over him. It didn't make sense that the stranger only wanted the lamp when there were riches enough here for a king. *Maybe he wants to save all the treasure for my mother and me*, Aladdin told himself. But as much as he wanted to believe that, it didn't feel true.

He started climbing the stairs. He could see light pouring from the desert sky illuminating the exit. "Is that you, boy?" The stranger commanded. "Did you find the lamp?"

Aladdin's uneasiness grew. The voice coming from above reminded him of the soldiers in the village. The voice of the stranger now sounded harsh and cruel.

"Yes," Aladdin replied. "I have the lamp."

"Give it to me," the stranger demanded.

Aladdin started climbing up the rope. "What are you doing?" the stranger yelled.

"I'm coming up!" Aladdin called back.

"No! You must tie the lamp to the rope. Once I have it, I'll throw the rope back down for you." A dark feeling swept through Aladdin. He felt that if he gave the stranger the lamp he would be abandoned underground.

"I don't think I can do that. The rope is thick and I can't tie it to the lamp. I've tucked the lamp in my tunic. When I climb up, I'll give it to you."

"Stupid boy!" the stranger yelled. "Wrap the rope around the lamp and send it to me, or I'll leave you there to die!"

"Curse you!" Aladdin shouted. "If you want the lamp, come get it yourself!" Aladdin wasn't sure where the words came from, but he knew they were brave.

"Fine! Die here then! I'll find another who will bring me the lamp."

Aladdin could see now that the stranger was an evil man and that he never intended to let Aladdin leave the chamber alive. "Are you there, boy? Are you there?" Aladdin sensed he shouldn't answer, and he moved away from the rope in case the stranger had some way of harming him. "Die then, you fool!" shouted the stranger as he pulled the rope up. Aladdin heard him murmur a few words, and the opening was soon covered by the large rock.

It was dark and quiet, and there was very little of his candle left. Aladdin was afraid to go back to the riches in case the stranger was telling the truth that to touch them was to die. He was thirsty and starting to feel hungry, but he had no food or water. His candle flickered and burned out. Aladdin couldn't see his hands or his feet.

He started to cry. "I'm sorry," he sobbed. "I'm sorry, Mother. I miss you, Father. I didn't mean to die in a stone chamber. I was only trying to help because we are so poor. I just wanted to do something for Mother and me." The more he thought about his plight the sadder he became. "I guess at least I'll see you soon, Dad," he spoke into the dark.

His tears fell on his tunic and cheeks. He wiped his face, and his hand brushed the lamp where more of his tears had fallen. He wiped the tears off. As his hand rubbed the lamp he felt a quiver. A loud WHOOSH erupted in the cave and Aladdin dropped the lamp in surprise as a large figure, more than double the boy's height, flowed from the lamp.

A warm glow lit the cave, and the treasure surrounding him glittered from the light surrounding the tall figure.

"Who are you?" gasped Aladdin.

"I am the genie of the lamp," he answered. "And you may have three wishes."

"How did you get here?"

"I serve whoever has the lamp." The genie looked at the lamp lying at Aladdin's feet. Aladdin quickly picked it up and secured it in his tunic.

"You're a genie?" Aladdin asked.

The genie looked at him quizzically. "Yes, Master. I am a genie."

"And you can do magic?"

"Yes, I can do magic," the genie replied. Although the genie's face was impassive, his eyes twinkled.

"Are you laughing at me, Genie?" Aladdin asked.

"No, Master."

"Then why are you smiling?"

"I'm sorry, master. I don't mean to offend you. You see, every master I have ever served receives three wishes, and when those wishes are complete our relationship ends. Almost every new master asks similar questions about whether I can do magic, or bring back the dead, or…"

"Wait! Can you bring back the dead? Can you bring back my father?"

"No," and for a moment the genie looked sad. "That power is forbidden even to me. Death is a land I cannot cross."

"Oh," Aladdin sighed. "That would have been my first wish…"

The cave was quiet. As quickly as the joy of the genie offering three wishes filled Aladdin with hope, the truth that nothing could bring his father back from the dead made him sad.

"Genie," Aladdin said slyly, "for my first wish I would like three more—"

"Three more wishes," the genie interrupted. "That is forbidden too. I can bring riches, fame, power and love, but you can't have infinite wishes or return anyone from the dead."

"Oh," Aladdin sighed. "It would have been nice to have three more wishes." The genie was silent as the treasure glittered from the light of the genie and the lamp."

"Do you know if there is any way out of here?" Aladdin asked.

The genie shook his head. "No, we are sealed inside, and there is no passage in or out."

"Can you free me from this place?"

"Of course! I'm a genie!"

"For my first wish I would like you to return me to my home and make sure my mother and I always have enough to eat."

"That sounds like two wishes."

"Not really," Aladdin protested. "Think of it this way. It's not so much that we are leaving here, you are magically taking me to my home that will now always have enough food for us to eat!" Aladdin grinned.

"So your first wish is for me to transport you to your home where you and your mother will always have enough to eat?"

"Yes, that is my wish."

The genie pondered for a moment and said, "Your wish is my command!"

The chamber grew bright as swirling lights and the sound of rushing air filled Aladdin's eyes and ears. He squeezed his eyes shut and held his breath. Soon the noise subsided, the light faded and Aladdin felt his feet on carpet. He opened his eyes and he was home! Fresh fruits, bread and honey were on the kitchen table. "Thank you, Genie!" he said. But there was no answer. The genie was gone.

He patted his tunic and felt the lamp. The fruit was fresh and sweet, the bread soft and warm and the honey the sweetest he had ever tasted. *This is wonderful.* Aladdin thought. *I can't wait to share this with my mother.*

The door opened and his mother stepped in. She looked tired, but smiled at Aladdin. "Hello, son," she said. "How was your day..." She gasped as she saw all the food. "Where did you get this?"

"I did a favor for a wealthy man, and in exchange he promised to make sure we are never hungry again. Isn't it wonderful, mother?" he said as he handed her a piece of bread. "Try some honey on it. It's really good!"

"Aladdin," she asked, "what really happened?"

"I told you. A wealthy man gave me this food, and he promised me we would never be hungry again."

"I don't believe you. But I'm too tried to argue and we need the food. Can you promise me you didn't steal it? I couldn't bear to lose you."

"I swear I didn't steal it."

"All right," she nodded. "We can talk more tomorrow. I'm going to change and then make us a meal fit for a king." Soon after dusk, his mother went to sleep and Aladdin stretched out on his bed and thought about the day.

I can have anything I want, he thought. *What should I ask the genie for next?* Aladdin's mind wandered from riches for himself and everyone he knew to living in a palace surrounded by his friends and beautiful young women. The more he fantasized about his next wish, the harder it was to decide. He felt fortunate, as if his luck had changed, and he fell peacefully asleep.

The next day, Aladdin awoke before dawn still excited by the possibilities of his next wish. As the sun slowly rose and covered the roads, houses and yards in an orange-red glow, Aladdin wandered the near empty streets feeling like the luckiest young man in the world.

Six soldiers with weapons drawn came toward him. Behind them were four muscular porters balancing an ornate golden litter on their shoulders. Thick red curtains enclosed the litter, and the warriors barely gave Aladdin a glance. One of the porters noticed Aladdin and ordered, "Turn down your eyes, boy! Don't you know it's forbidden to look at the princess?"

Aladdin's heart leaped at being so close to the princess, but he knew he could be whipped or worse if he didn't heed the warning. He watched the feet of the soldiers and porters pass by.

A small fan fell directly in front of Aladdin, and a voice called out, "Stop! I've dropped my fan!" The porter's feet halted, and the soldiers turned around.

Without thinking, Aladdin picked up the fan and raised it up toward the litter. The most beautiful face he had ever seen smiled back at him. She had rich brown eyes and an olive complexion. Her lips were full and firm, and her dark hair long and luxuriant. A terrible feeling grew in Aladdin's stomach, and the smile he gave the princess faded. *What have I done!* He thought. *It's forbidden to look at the princess!*

The princess's smile faded too as they both realized what could happen to Aladdin for seeing her.

"Your highness!" The captain of the soldiers said. "This boy has looked at you. We will arrest him and ask the king what punishment he wants imposed."

Thinking quickly, the princess answered, "There is no need for that captain. My servants are all exempt from my father's command that no men look at me until I am married and, as you can see, this young man is serving me by retrieving my fan." She reached her hand from the litter and took the fan from Aladdin's hand. Her fingers were soft, and Aladdin shuddered as she touched him. She looked directly into Aladdin's eyes. "Of course, now his short service to me is over and if he were to continue looking at me, you must follow my father's command."

The captain looked sharply at Aladdin, but he had already returned his eyes to the ground. "Consider yourself lucky, boy," he growled. "Let's get going, men," he ordered.

Aladdin imagined that the princess smiled at him as she left, but he didn't dare look up until the sound of the soldiers' and porters' footsteps faded. When he raised his eyes all he could see was the back of the princess's litter far down the road. His heart felt broken. She was the most beautiful young woman he had ever seen.

That night after dinner, Aladdin asked, "Mother, do you know who will marry the princess?"

"A king or a noble, I suppose. The best would be a prince, but I don't know of an eligible one."

"How does she choose who to marry?" Aladdin asked.

His mother laughed, "She doesn't. The king chooses her suitors and husband. Most kings want to find a prince. Because the princess is the king's only child, and the queen died when she was born, whoever marries the princess is likely to become our king. Why do you ask?"

"If I tell you something, do you promise not to tell anyone?" Aladdin asked. His mother nodded. "Today I saw the princess!"

"How could you? You could be in great trouble!"

"No, it's okay. I was on the street, and she was concealed in her litter, but when she passed me her fan fell. I was looking down like I'm supposed to so I saw it hit the ground. I returned it to her and, because I was her servant for a few minutes, I got to see her."

"You were very fortunate you weren't arrested. What did she look like?"

"She was the most beautiful girl I've ever seen." Aladdin sighed.

"I'm sure she was, but you must forget about her. She is destined for a prince or a king, and we are ordinary people."

"I know," Aladdin agreed. "But it's hard to forget seeing

a girl so beautiful, and when she touched my hand…"

"She touched you?" his mother gasped.

"Yes, when I handed her the fan. It was like butterflies started flying in my stomach!"

"Oh, Aladdin," his mother embraced him. "I'm happy you got to see the princess, but you must let this go. She's not for you."

"I know," Aladdin murmured. "She can only marry a prince." A smiled crossed Aladdin's face as he realized that his wish to become a prince and marry the princess could come true. All he had to do was ask the genie of the lamp.

The next morning, Aladdin woke up thinking of the princess. He grabbed the lamp and gently rubbed it. A loud WHOOSH filled the room, and the genie towered over him.

"Hello," the genie said. "How can I serve the master of the lamp?"

"Genie," Aladdin asked. "Can you make me a prince? I want to marry the princess, and the only way her father the king will see me as fit for her is if I am a prince."

"So you wish to marry her?"

"Yes!" said Aladdin. "She is the most beautiful woman I have ever seen."

"I can make you a prince. Even more, I can bring you riches and gold and an entourage of servants so you can go to the castle and ask the king for his daughter's hand in marriage."

"That's perfect, Genie! Thank you!"

"So is that your second wish?" the genie asked. "To become a prince so you can prepare to marry the princess?"

"Yes, that is my wish."

A swirling cloud appeared before Aladdin's eyes. He felt his clothes growing lighter and different on his skin. As the cloud receded, he felt himself riding on a powerful, white stallion. In front of him, richly dressed servants rode their horses and tossed coins along their path. "Make way for the prince!" they shouted.

Crowds pressed in to grab the coins and to see the handsome, young prince astride the stallion. As they approached the castle, the gates were flung open. One of Aladdin's servants approached the king's vizier and said, "The great Prince Aladdin has come to ask the king for his daughter's hand in marriage."

The vizier looked at the servants, the finery and Aladdin and bowed deeply. "Welcome, your grace, welcome. Let me inform the king of your arrival."

Soon Aladdin was taken before the king. Aladdin's servants placed chests of gold, jewels and treasures before the throne, and the king was stunned by Aladdin's wealth.

"Your majesty," Aladdin said. "All the world knows that the finest princess in all the lands is your daughter. I come before you and beg that you grant me her royal hand in marriage."

The king shifted in his seat. He didn't know this prince, but he was handsome, rich and well-spoken. Knowing of no other comparable suitors, the king answered, "Prince

Aladdin, I grant your request for my daughter's hand in marriage, and my hope is that you will enjoy many happy years together."

Aladdin beamed in excitement, "Thank you, your majesty. I will do all I can to prove worthy of your trust." The two men smiled at each other as the courtiers murmured and gossiped about the handsome young prince now betrothed to their princess.

News of the wedding reached the ears of the stranger, and he knew that the prince was Aladdin. The stranger was really an evil magician. Realizing that Aladdin had discovered the secret of the genie of the lamp, he cast a spell to see where Aladdin lived, in hopes he might recover the lamp for himself.

He disguised himself as a merchant and knocked on Aladdin's mother's door. When she answered, he said, "New lamps for old, good woman, new lamps for old," and he held up some beautiful, ornate lamps for her to see.

"Why, those are lovely. Why are you giving new lamps for old?"

The merchant shrugged, "My master has customers who want antiques, so he has sent me to find fortunate women such as yourself who can trade an old lamp for a new one."

"I think we have some old lamps," she said as she remembered seeing the old brass lamp in Aladdin's room. "Would this do?" she asked, returning with Aladdin's lamp.

"Of course, of course. It is an old lamp, and for this you

may have any new lamp I own." She carefully selected an ornate lamp with a small red jewel. "My son will love this one. Thank you!"

"My pleasure," the merchant said as he shuffled down the road.

When Aladdin came home that night his mother immediately noticed the change in his appearance. "There is something different about you," she said.

"Please, mother. Sit down," and he told her about the stranger and the riches from his father and how the stranger locked him underground to die, but then he discovered the genie in the lamp.

As Aladdin continued to tell the story, his mother felt uneasy. "And that is how we got all the food," he continued. "My second wish was to be a prince so I could marry the princess, and now I am! You are now the mother of a prince, and we will live in a castle and never worry about money or food again. I don't know what I'm going to do with my third wish..."

"Aladdin," his mother interrupted, "Earlier today a merchant came down the street offering new lamps for old. I remembered seeing that old lamp in your room, and I traded it to him for a beautiful new one. I didn't know and I was trying to please you. I am so sorry!"

"Oh, Mother!" Aladdin cried as he went to his room and returned with the new lamp. "Do you know where his shop is?"

She shook her head. "I have never seen him before."

"We must find him!" Aladdin said, and he and his mother set out walking the streets and looking for the merchant who was really the evil magician. Hours later, they returned home, tired and dejected.

"It's okay, Mother," Aladdin said trying to comfort her. "You were only trying to help me, and at least I am free from the cave, we will always have food and now I'm marrying the princess."

"You're a good boy, Aladdin," she said. They went to sleep. The next morning things didn't seem so bad. The king was making plans for the wedding, and Aladdin was so happy about his marriage to the princess that he didn't worry too much about the wish he lost. Instead he thought about his future life with the princess and how happy they could be together.

On the wedding day, the palace was filled with royal guests, family and friends. Aladdin and his mother had everything they needed for the wedding. The genie's magic continued even though the lamp was gone.

When Aladdin saw the princess, his heart leaped. She was the most beautiful woman he had ever seen. Nothing on earth, not the setting sun, the melody of songbirds or the colors of the rainbow could match her beauty to him. When their eyes met, he felt she loved him as much as he loved her and he vowed at that moment to always be faithful and true to her.

As they stood in front of the crowd, almost husband and wife, the officiant said, "Does anyone here know of any reason that these two should not be wed? Speak now, or forever hold your peace." Aladdin turned to her and smiled knowing in a few moments they would be married.

"Hearing no objection, I now…"

"I OBJECT!" A loud voice cut through the crowd as a well-dressed older man pushed his way to the front. "I object because the princess is to be my bride!"

"Seize him!" the king shouted. But as the king's guards moved toward him, they froze.

"Fools! Do you think you can stop me with mere mortal ways? Surely you recognize me, Aladdin?" Aladdin saw that it was the stranger. "And perhaps your mother will recognize me too as she was so kind to give me this lamp!" Aladdin's heart sank as the magician pulled the lamp from under his robes and waved it for all to see.

"Since we are gathered here for a wedding, let's have the ceremony proceed. But not with this imposter," he pointed toward Aladdin. "But with me." He rubbed the lamp and the genie appeared larger than Aladdin had ever seen him. "Genie of the lamp, my wish is to be the king and bridegroom now!"

"Your wish is my command," the genie said. The king's crown shifted to the magician's head, and Aladdin's robes fell on the magician's shoulder.

"Now let the wedding proceed," the magician commanded. The princess looked horrified. Her eyes pleaded with Aladdin for help.

"Wait!" shouted Aladdin.

"I will kill you, boy," the magician threatened.

"No, wait! I'm trying to help you! You want to be the most important man in the world, isn't that right?"

"Yes," he agreed.

"But you are only a king! The genie can make you the most important person in the world, all you have to do is ask."

"Is that true, Genie?" the magician demanded. "Can you make me the most important person in the world?"

"Yes, master. It is true."

"Then I command you to make me the most important person in the world—and do it right now!"

"As you wish, Master," the genie replied, and the magician started shrinking. The lines on his face became smooth, the beard on his cheeks withdrew in his chin and his stature became shorter and shorter until finally a young child lay curled on the floor next to the princess with the lamp beside him.

"It's a baby," the princess gasped. "But how?" she asked Aladdin.

"He thought that the most important person alive is a king, but it isn't. Before my father died he always told me that I was the most important person in the world. He said that every baby is the promise of the future. Men and women grow old and die. Their minds fade and their bodies ache as they age, but a child is the promise of the future for all of us," Aladdin said.

"Your father was a wise man, and you are wise to heed

him," the king said. "When I am gone, I know you will make a good king."

"Aladdin," his mother reminded him as she looked toward the lamp, "you still have one more wish. Perhaps you should make it now."

Aladdin picked up the lamp as the genie still hovered over them. "Genie," Aladdin commanded, "I want to make my third and final wish."

"Yes, master," the genie replied.

"I wish that beauty may never die in this world."

"Your wish is my command, master." A gentleness washed over the crowd as the flowers became a little more colorful, the sky glowed a little bluer, all the clothing looked a little prettier, and the sun seemed to shine a little brighter. As he smiled at Aladdin, the genie returned to the lamp.

Aladdin became a good king. He and the princess lived for many more years, always surrounded by beauty and the love of their family and friends.

As the story begins, Aladdin is a fatherless boy seeking his place in the world. His mother knows she can't directly help him the way she could when he was younger. He has outgrown his willingness to listen to her without questioning what she says. Moreover, Aladdin is experiencing the cultural and spiritual legacy of all adolescents, which is an instinct to separate from their parents so they can become independent, mature and capable of living in the world on their own.

All children need to learn to mind their caregivers when they are young. Parents caution their offspring not to place themselves in harm's way and offer protection from the dangers of the world that they have learned from their own life experience. It isn't appropriate to negotiate with a five-year-old about swimming alone in the ocean. Instead, the mother sometimes tells her young son, "You can't do that, because I said so."

But as the five-year-old grows to a teenager and physical maturity emerges, it becomes more appropriate for a young teenager to question, negotiate and start to learn to interact with the world on their own.

It doesn't serve a teenager to overly rely on a parent. The role of the parent of a teenager is to begin to let go of protecting the child and to teach the child to protect himself. Good parents don't force their child to grow up the way they think they should be. Good parents teach their children to become who they really are.

In most families, it is a difficult time, as old roles die, new roles are not yet established, and mothers and fathers feel betrayed and unappreciated while their sons or daughters feel stifled. This process often feels painful, awkward and frustrating.

One way to help move through this necessary stage is for parents to encourage the sometimes painful growth and development of their child, with the knowledge that the difficulties of the present circumstances will subside as their sons or daughters mature.

It is inevitable that in their development, adolescents will make mistakes. When the stranger appears and offers to take Aladdin to a treasure left by his father, Aladdin doesn't consider that the man might be a predator. He mistook a man who would kill him to be his father's best friend. That which we want most earnestly, we believe most easily.

The lamp symbolizes the mysterious, often plain-looking treasure that is not recognized and valued for its true worth. Aladdin didn't know that the lamp was the most valuable thing in the chamber! In stories and in life, our most valuable gifts often don't immediately reveal their value. Many of our greatest gifts and resources are wrapped in the appearance of the ordinary. Because of that, it can be difficult to discern their true worth.

The first steps to reclaiming and using the gift of intuition is to look for it, learn to recognize it and then start using it. It took Aladdin a little while to realize that the lamp was the most valuable thing in the cave, but when he discovered its gifts, that awareness changed everything.

The same is true for us. Once we learn to recognize and use the gifts of our inner world, it can help us wisely navigate the world we wake up in everyday. Our lives aren't the same. We have powerful resources. We gain hope.

Like Aladdin, we still make mistakes and can be

driven by visions of riches, and overwhelming desires for an attractive partner, fame and power. But once we reclaim and use the gift of intuition, we have a greater capacity to learn from our mistakes. A metamorphosis occurs as our life experience merges with the growing wisdom that comes with using our intuition, and we begin to become a whole person. We start to live our potential and understand who we really are.

Most of us believe that magic lamps exist only in fairy tales and that the banal world of everyday life doesn't have magic lamps, fairy godmothers, guardian angels, heroes or dragons.

This belief keeps us from searching for the magic lamps in our lives, yet they exist as surely as stars are in the sky, whether we can see them or not. Everything in fairy tales, heroic movies and long-forgotten childhood play exists somewhere. There is magic and mystery in the world, and it's usually much closer than we know. Sometimes we need only to remember and desire what we once possessed for it to be reclaimed.

Chapter Five

COURAGE

Once we have a sense of our destiny and begin to reclaim our intuition, we have enough insight to begin our quest to discover who we really are and what we are uniquely here to do.

To take the next step and begin our journey requires courage. This courage is deeper than what many of us think of as what being brave means.

Courage comes from facing our fears, even when we feel afraid to face them. This is the courage of showing up when we are afraid we will fail and of pushing forward even when it feels like all is lost. It is behaving bravely despite feeling afraid, and going forward despite feeling fearful. It is the courage of heroes.

The odd thing about courage is that it often comes when fear feels strongest. One of the reasons it is so important to learn to walk with a dragon is that dragons will walk alongside us through fears. We feel braver when there is a dragon by our side!

There are many forms of cowardice and many forms of bravery. Some of the most soul-crippling, personally devastating and shame-inducing cowardice isn't obvious to others. These include not standing up for a friend who is being attacked when they aren't there to defend themselves, or laughing at or telling "funny" jokes that make fun of others.

The shame that comes when we violate our summons to courageously lend our voice to what we believe in, what is true to our soul, can be the most debilitating shame of all. Once we allow that, it's a short journey to feeling worthless, unloved and that the world would be a better place if we didn't live in it.

Many of the journeys that require the greatest courage aren't the obvious journeys that others can see. They are the quests we take to be true to ourselves. They are the times we become willing to risk showing our truth, expressing our values and beliefs and accepting others may reject us for our courage.

Acceptance from others can't be purchased with the coin of vapid platitudes, silence that implies consent, or disingenuous agreements that violate our core sense of justice.

Adolescents try this frequently, as their desire to "fit in," "belong" or "be popular" is often so intense that some are willing to almost trade their souls to alleviate the anxiety and pain that compels them to desperately seek acceptance from their peers.

As powerful as this destructive motivation to betray ourselves to fit in can be, what truly fills the need we have for love, acceptance and a feeling of belonging isn't the approbation of our peers. It is receiving love and respect from ourselves and the kinship of dragons.

Because dragons are magical beasts, they don't always take the forms so often used to describe them. A dragon can appear as a dragonfly, an eagle, a fish, a cat, a dog, a cow, a horse, or in any form it chooses to take. Because the natural home of the dragon is a world different than this one, dragons instinctively know which form to take to be most helpful to us in our journeys. My dragon sometimes took the form of a dog, but I knew he was my dragon.

In the well-known story of *Jack and the Beanstalk*, Jack has to face his fears and confront what terrifies him. He displays remarkable courage, not because he isn't afraid, but because he keeps going despite his fear. As you read this story, look for his "dragon." Is it the beanstalk? The harp? The cow? Or does the dragon simply live within Jack? Even though his "dragon" isn't readily visible and Jack may not always be conscious of it, not being aware of your dragon doesn't mean that it isn't there.

The advantage of seeing, communicating with and creating a conscious relationship with your dragon, is that you will be stronger, wiser and better able to deal with the inevitable challenges of your journey.

Something important to know about dragons is that sometimes men want their dragon to help them find the woman or man of their dreams, or help acquire vast sums of money, or gain power over others. Healthy dragons generally aren't interested in money, sex, power or many of the superficial things that can create such enticing but wrongful lusts in human beings.

Dragons are interested in justice. When we are engaged in confronting that which isn't right—injustice, abuse and evil—dragons are engaged in our cause. Dragons understand the importance of friendship, family, duty, loyalty and oaths of fealty. They abhor betrayal.

What motivates and inspires a dragon isn't always what motivates men, but it is wise to consider that often it should be.

JACK AND THE BEANSTALK

Once upon a time, a boy named Jack and his mother lived in great poverty on a small farm not far from a village. Jack wasn't really lazy, but he wasn't industrious either. The extent of his efforts to help himself and his mother depended mostly on his mood. On days that he felt mature and responsible, and recognized the importance of contributing to his family, he worked hard and his mother was proud of him. On days he felt self-indulgent, lazy and tired, his mother couldn't find him, and she worried constantly.

Jack always wondered what had happened to his father. His mother told him his father was murdered, but she wouldn't say more no matter how much he pressed her. There were still signs of his dad in their home: a leather hunting jacket hung in a closet, a woolen cap, and a table that his mother often mentioned his father had carved for her when they were first married.

On days his mother was gone, Jack often tried on the jacket and hat. He felt so small in the large jacket whose sleeves extended farther than his fingertips and in the hat that drooped over his forehead and covered his eyes. As Jack grew older, he noticed that his hand could now reach through the end of the sleeve of his father's jacket and the woolen cap no longer covered his eyes. *Someday I'll fit in his clothes.* Jack thought. *And when I do, I'll find out what happened to my father and avenge him.*

Jack and his mother never had enough money to buy new shoes or clothes. What little they had was spent buying food, but Jack often went to bed hungry. His mother tried to supplement the meager food they grew in their yard by cleaning and washing clothes for others. But even though she worked hard and was almost always tired, her efforts produced very little money.

One day Jack's mother said, "I'm sorry it has come to this, but we have to sell the cow."

"We can't! We can't sell the cow!" Jack protested. "We won't have any milk then!"

"I'm sorry," she sighed. "But the cow is so thin she isn't producing milk now anyway, and we have no money to feed her." Jack knew it was true. The cow hadn't given milk in weeks, and he could see the bones protruding through her skin.

"Do you want me to help, Mother?"

"What can you do?" she asked.

"I could take her to the market and make sure we get everything we can for her."

"I don't know, Jack," she said dubiously. "You aren't experienced at selling at the market and some of the folks there are awfully good at taking advantage of others' misfortune."

"I can do it! I've been watching men at the market for a long time now, and I promise I can get a good price for her. Please let me go, Mother."

"All right," she sighed. "But be wise, Jack. Please. This is all we have and we need this money to eat."

"I will. Thank you for trusting me, Mom."

The next morning Jack woke up and took their cow down the road toward the market. It was a warm, sunny day, and Jack felt like a grown-up as he led the cow down the road and thought about how much money he could get for her.

He almost didn't notice the old woman sitting on a log as he passed by.

"Good morning, young man," she cackled.

Jack was startled. "Good morning," he stammered. He paused and looked at the woman. She seemed very old with a hooked nose, greasy hair and a dirty brown shawl.

But she smiled at him, and that made him feel good.

"What brings you and this beautiful animal out on this fine day?"

"I'm glad you think she's a beautiful animal," Jack answered. "I'm on my way to sell her at the market. We have had enough of her, and my mother sent me to sell her," he bragged.

The old woman nodded. "I see, I see." She stepped up to the cow and petted her. "Why is she so thin?"

"We don't have enough food for her," Jack admitted.

"Hard times…these are hard times," the old woman said. "You must sell her because you and your mother can't afford to feed her and you need the money?"

Jack felt embarrassed and didn't want to admit the truth, but despite that he said, "Yes, that is why we have to sell her."

"You're a good boy to help your mother, and a brave boy to tell me the truth," the old woman said. "Well, Jack, this is your lucky day. I am going to help you and your mother. I have something very special and magical, and I was trying to decide who I should share it with. After hearing of you and your mother's plight, I have decided to help you." She reached in her pocket. "Hold out your hand," she commanded. Jack did as he was told. He felt her drop a handful of small objects in his palm.

"These are magic beans," she whispered. "When you go home tonight, plant them in the light of the moon. When you wake up in the morning you will see something astonishing that will change you and your mother's lives for the better." Jack closed his fist, and the beans felt almost as if they were alive and moving.

"Thank you for giving them to me," Jack replied.

"Giving them! I'm not giving them to you," the old woman laughed. "I am trading them to you for your cow." Jack felt an odd feeling of worry growing in his stomach.

"I don't know—my mother is expecting me to bring her back money for the cow." The beans were moving in his clinched hand, and he knew he wanted to keep them.

"Don't worry, Jack. Your mother will be proud of you. When she sees that you traded the cow for something more valuable than money—that you have magic beans— she will be very happy." Jack nodded in agreement.

"I'll do it!" he said. As he spoke those words he felt that something important had happened, and he put the beans in his pocket for safekeeping as he gave the cow to the old woman.

"Don't forget, Jack," the old woman called as he turned to walk back home. "Plant the beans in the light of the moon, and receive your reward."

As Jack walked home, he began to doubt his decision. He worried that his mother might be disappointed. Even though the old woman said the beans were magic, they looked ordinary. The closer he got to home, the more he worried that his mother might not approve.

"How did it go, Jack?" His mother called as she eagerly waited at the window for him to come home. "Did you get a good price for her?"

"I think so," Jack stammered. "But I didn't sell her so much as trade her."

His mother's face grew taut. "Traded for what?" she asked.

Jack put his hands in his pocket and felt the small bundle the old woman had given him. The hope and excitement he felt on the road evaporated as his fingers clasped the small, round beans. He pulled the bundle out and showed his mother. "For these, Mom. I traded for these."

"What are they?"

"They are magic beans."

"Beans? Magic beans?" Her voice rose in anger and the pain and worry on her face grew. "Please don't tell me you traded the only thing we owned of any value for some worthless beans!"

"They aren't worthless beans," he yelled. "They are magic beans."

"I'm sure that's what someone told you, and you were dumb enough to believe them," his mother yelled. "I hope they are magic enough to fill your stomach because that's all we have to eat."

"I'm sorry, Mom," Jack called as his mother went to her room, slammed the door and didn't reply. "I'm sorry, Mom," he muttered. He hated the feeling of disappointing her. He worried that she was right, that the old woman had taken advantage of him and that the beans were worthless. *There is only one way to know for sure*, he told himself.

Later that night, he went outside and carefully followed the old woman's directions. He planted the beans in the moonlight. When he was done, he patted the earth, gave the planting a blessing and went inside to sleep.

Jack awoke with a start. "Jack, Jack!" his mother yelled. "Hurry and come outside." Pulling his feet from under the covers, Jack rubbed his eyes and went out the front door. A shadow fell across their small house as a giant beanstalk, wider than Jack or his mother, blocked the morning light.

"It was true," he murmured. "They were magic beans."

"I'm sorry I didn't believe you, Jack." She put her arm around his shoulder. "How tall do you think it is?"

"I don't know. It goes past the clouds."

"What an amazing thing," his mother said. "I'm sorry I didn't believe you," she apologized.

"It's okay. I started to wonder myself!"

"Did she tell you what you should do with the beanstalk?" his mother asked.

Jack shrugged. "Not exactly, but I think she meant for me to climb it."

The beanstalk stretched to the sky and, as Jack started climbing, he said, "I love you, Mom. I'll do my best to make you proud!"

Jack climbed and he climbed. The beanstalk was warm to his touch and at times it almost felt it was growing as he climbed. Soon he passed through the clouds and the view of his house faded until all he could see were clouds below him, blue sky surrounding him and a large dark cloud directly above him that the beanstalk disappeared into.

As Jack passed through the large cloud, he thought he heard voices. As he kept climbing, he realized he heard the babbling of water and the chirping of birds. Cautiously, he placed his foot through the mist swirling around the beanstalk. His foot rested firmly against something hard. *Here goes nothing* Jack thought as he let go of the beanstalk and took a step.

The ground was solid and as Jack stepped away from the beanstalk, he saw he was in a land similar to his own but different. The sun was brighter, and there were no signs of people. A broad road, at least three times as wide as the road from his farm to the market extended ahead. On either side of the road, rich fields of giant vegetables grew in rows. Jack decided to follow the highway and though the sky was bright, the earth warm, and the plants rich and green, he felt a sense of uneasiness as he walked down the road.

He passed over a hill and on the other side was a large stone castle. The archways were more than three times Jack's height, and his fear grew as he approached the castle. The courtyard door was open. Though no one was there, Jack felt certain the castle wasn't abandoned. The smell of fresh baked bread caught his attention, and he followed the scent to a kitchen.

His eyes drifted to a large table in the center of the stone room. Jack could barely reach the table top, but he pulled himself up and discovered two loaves of bread as large as his leg cooling on the table. Realizing he was hungry, Jack broke a piece of bread from the cooling loaf. Looking around, he realized everything was at least three times larger than any kitchen he had ever seen. A spoon resting on the table was larger than his mother's garden trowel, and the stove looked big enough to serve his village. Near the spoon was a goblet the size of a bucket, and the chair looked large enough to seat a giant.

"Hurry now, or the bread will be cold," a loud voice called from the courtyard. Looking around quickly, Jack hid in a bread box. It was just large enough for him to curl inside, and through a crack he could see the kitchen. An enormous woman came into the room. Behind her walked an even larger man. He was three heads taller than Jack, and the ground shook when he stepped in the room.

"I want more than bread," the giant yelled. "Bring me some meat!"

"You know I've got no meat today," she said.

"A giant can't live on vegetables and bread!" he complained. The giant stopped a moment and sniffed. "Do you smell that?" he asked.

"Smell what?"

"That odor it's almost like I'm smelling a man—"

"There's no man here. You're just thinking that because you're hungry."

"No! I can smell him! FEE-FI-FO-FUM! I smell the blood of a human man. Be he alive or be he dead, I'll grind his bones to make my bread!"

"You're imagining things because you're hungry. There hasn't been a man here in an age."

"Well, who ate this then?" the giant asked, pointing to the loaf where Jack had taken some bread.

"Probably a bird," she said.

"I know the smell of a man, and I'm telling you one has been here."

"Suit yourself," she shrugged. "If you find him, let me know and I'll bake him into a pie."

The giant started eating his bread. "I'll bet he came to steal my treasure," he grumbled.

"No one is stealing your treasure," she assured him. "Your goose lays a golden egg every day, and I save them all right here," she said pointing to a basket Jack hadn't noticed on the counter across the table. "And your harp plays the most beautiful music anyone has ever heard."

"Bring me my harp," the giant demanded. The giantess opened a cupboard and brought out a harp. The body was made of gold, and its iridescent strings twinkled as she set the harp on the table.

"Play!" commanded the giant. The most beautiful melody Jack had ever heard rose from the strings. The harp had a carved face, and when Jack watched it, he could see the eyes, nose and mouth moving. It was a magic harp, and he knew he needed to bring it to his mother. *This is why I'm here*, he realized. *I need to bring this harp home.* As the music continued to play, Jack almost forgot the danger he was in.

When the song ended and the giantess put the harp away, Jack could see the sadness in the harp's eyes.

"All mine, all mine," the giant said. "No one can ever listen to her but me."

"Let's put the bread away, and I'll help you gather some vegetables for dinner," the giantess said.

Jack was terrified. He was hiding in the bread box, and if she opened it he would be fully exposed.

"No, take it with us. I'm famished and harvesting is hungry work." Nodding, she wrapped the bread in a cloth and the two of them left the kitchen.

Jack knew he was in great danger, but he also remembered the old woman telling him that the beans would lead him to his reward. He carefully climbed out of the breadbox, lowered himself to the floor, climbed up to the counter and looked in the basket where the giantess kept the golden eggs. The eggs were large, and Jack fit all he could in his pockets. He wanted to take the harp but he didn't know how he could carry the harp and the gold.

I'll take the gold first and come back for the harp next time. As Jack climbed down the kitchen counter the corner of his pocket tore and one of the golden eggs fell to the stone floor with a crash. Without looking back, Jack ran out of the kitchen, across the courtyard and sprinted as fast as he could to the swirling mist that surrounded the beanstalk. He didn't think the giant had seen him, but without taking any chances he leaped to the beanstalk and climbed down as fast as he could.

When he reached the ground, it was nighttime and

the moon lit the small yard surrounding their cottage. He hurried in the house and went to his mother's bed.

"I'm home," he whispered. His mother hugged him and tears filled her eyes.

"I was so worried you wouldn't make it back," she sobbed. "If anything had happened to you I couldn't have survived it. It was bad enough losing your father but to lose you too—" her voice trailed off.

"What happened to my father?" Jack asked. "I think I'm old enough to know."

"Oh, Jack. I've tried to protect you and keep it from you."

"Please, Mother. I need to know."

She was quiet for a moment, her face lightly lit by the moonlight coming through her bedroom window. "Your father was killed by a giant. There was a terrible storm, and lightning and thunder filled the sky for hours. In the middle of it, a giant, at least three times as large as your father, appeared in the village. No one knew where he came from. He stole a harp from the church and a goose from the mayor. People said the goose was magic and could lay golden eggs, and the harp played the most beautiful sounds anyone had ever heard.

"Your father and some of the village men tried to stop him, but the giant beat them like they were little children. Your father wasn't one of the lucky ones. The giant knocked him senseless, and when they brought him home he couldn't speak, or open his eyes. I tried to squeeze his hand and tell him I loved him, but I'm not even sure if he squeezed my hand back or I imagined it."

She was very quiet. The room was dark, still, and Jack listened without interrupting. "Three days later, he took his last breath and died."

"Why didn't you tell me?" Jack asked.

"I didn't want you to be afraid. I didn't want you to ever think your father was weak."

"Why would I think my father was weak when he died at the hands of a giant? It wasn't a fair fight! I've seen the giant, Mother, and I'm going to kill him."

"No, Jack!" she gasped. "Let it go, or he will kill you too."

"I don't think so. I think that old woman who gave me the magic beans was there to help me avenge my father. The giant is evil. He killed my father, and he will kill again if he can. I have to get rid of him."

"Oh, Jack. I wish you could let it go. How can risking your life be good for you and our family?"

"For some reason, Mother, I know this is mine to do. So, I'll do the best I can, and now that I know the truth, I can make a plan. Here, Mother, I brought some golden eggs from the giant. Maybe we can use them to help get what I need to kill him."

Jack didn't sleep well. His mind kept thinking of ways to kill the giant. He considered poisoning, but couldn't think how he could get enough poison up the beanstalk and then find a way for the giant to eat it. He knew he couldn't beat him with a sword, a club or his hands. Even an arrow from Jack's bow was more likely to annoy the giant than to injure him.

Jack's mother took one of the eggs to the market, and for the first time in many years their cupboards were filled with food and Jack and his mother had new coats and shoes.

About a week after Jack returned, he had a dream. In the dream, he felt terrified as he ran from the castle, down the road toward the beanstalk, with the giant chasing him. He climbed down the beanstalk as fast as he could with the giant pursuing him. When he reached the bottom, his mother handed him his father's axe, "Hurry, Jack. Hurry!" she yelled.

Jack could see the beanstalk swaying from the weight of the giant, but his axe was true and he chopped down the beanstalk. The giant fell with a great crash, and when Jack and his mother approached the body they could see he was dead.

That's what I must do thought Jack when he awoke. I need to lure the giant to the beanstalk and then reach the bottom and cut it down while he is still high enough that the fall will kill him.

Jack decided to spend a month preparing. He ran for hours a day. After the first week, he started carrying a large pack filled with rocks to simulate the weight of the harp and the goose, for he wanted to rescue them too.

To practice agility, he climbed hundreds of feet up and

down the beanstalk every day. His mother watched him with growing anxiety, "Be careful, Jack!" she warned.

"I will," he answered. But despite what he told his mother he knew that if he didn't almost fly down the beanstalk the giant would kill him.

The night before he returned to the giant's castle, Jack had another dream. In this dream the old woman who gave him the beans appeared to him in the moonlight. Jack knew he was dreaming, yet it almost seemed that the dream was happening on this very night. The same moon that appeared in the sky when he went to sleep was shining in the dream and the cool air breeze felt exactly the same in the dream as it did when Jack went to sleep.

"You've done well, but it isn't enough, Jack," she warned him. "You won't have time to chop down the beanstalk, and you haven't practiced it. You are fleet of foot and can run fast. You are quick climbing down the beanstalk, but if you follow your plan, you will die."

"What else can I do?" Jack cried. "I've done all I know to do."

"You must chop through the beanstalk before you climb it, leaving only a small part of it intact. The only way you will have enough time to make the giant fall and die is if the beanstalk is almost chopped down."

"But how will I know if enough is enough?" Jack asked.

"You are smart and must trust yourself. You have spent your whole life in nature, you have chopped many trees for firewood. In a few minutes you will wake up, and you must go outside right now and chop the beanstalk as far as you can, making sure it is still strong enough to hold you and the giant when he chases you down."

"You can't tell me how far I must cut it?"

"No, it's for you to decide."

Jack awoke in a cold sweat. He looked out his window and saw the beanstalk. The night appeared exactly as it did in his dream except the old woman was gone.

He quietly put on his pants, shoes and new coat. As he left the house, he picked up his father's axe. When he approached the beanstalk, it looked immense. He understood now it would take many blows to bring it down.

He ran his fingers along the blade of the axe. His father had always kept it sharp, and Jack did too. *Help me, Father,* Jack whispered into the night. *Help me cut deep enough to kill the giant, but shallow enough that I can survive.* Feeling the strength of his father and ancestors coursing through him, Jack swung the axe against the base of the beanstalk. He struck low and the beanstalk shuddered as a small piece flew off.

THWACK! The axe sounded as it penetrated the beanstalk. THWACK! THWACK! THWACK! The axe and Jack and the beanstalk were in a rhythm now. It almost felt like a dance. Jack kept swinging, the axe landed true, and the beanstalk swayed in the night almost as if it was helping Jack to defeat the giant.

The light receded as the moon set, and Jack felt the axe lighten as he reduced the intensity of his blows. A large pile of the beanstalk surrounded him, and though it still stood, Jack knew it wasn't too strong now.

I hope it's enough, he murmured as he ceased swinging the axe. He carefully picked up all the pieces of beanstalk he removed and placed them near the barn. They felt wet and moist in his hand.

With a feeling of completion, he wiped the axe blade clean and returned to his house and bed. When he awoke the next morning, the sky was sunny, the air was fresh, and the crisp feeling of autumn was in the air. His mother had made him breakfast. Even though he wasn't hungry, he forced himself to eat. His mother silently watched him, tears forming in her eyes.

"I don't know what I'll do if something..."

"It's okay, Mother," Jack interrupted. "A coward dies a thousand deaths, a hero only one. I think I will come home and kill the giant, but I know I'm doing what I was born to do. If it wasn't for you, I wouldn't be able to do it." He got up from the table and embraced her tightly. "I love you," he said.

"I love you, too," she answered.

"It's time. You know what to do?" he asked.

"Watch the sky and, as soon as I see you, stand by the base of the beanstalk with your father's axe. The moment your feet land on the ground, I'll hand it to you."

"That's it," Jack said. "I'll see you soon." He picked up

his empty backpack and strapped it over his shoulders as he left the house and started climbing.

He climbed and he climbed and he climbed and he climbed. He went through the first bank of clouds and, when he approached the cloud and swirling mist that he now knew concealed the giant's castle, he offered a silent prayer. *Help me, Father,* he said.

This time he set his foot solidly on the ground and began to walk toward the giant's castle. Jack's plan was to capture the goose who laid the golden eggs, rescue the harp and then let the giant see him and start chasing him to the beanstalk. What he didn't know was how he could delay the giant's seeing him until he was as far away as possible and gain a long enough head start to avoid the giant's catching him.

Jack made his way to the castle, silently entered the courtyard and made his way toward the kitchen. He heard a loud HONK! and turning he saw a goose in a cage. Unlike most things in the giant's land, the goose was the size of a goose back home. He placed his hand in the cage and stroked her. "Are you the goose that lays the golden eggs?" he asked. There was no answer. "I guess it doesn't matter," he said. I only have room for one goose, and I'm not leaving you here to get eaten by the giant if you're a regular goose. Can you please stay silent in my pack?" Jack asked. "Look, I made a hole for you to look out and breath." Jack wiggled his fingers through the cut he made in the pack. Jack reached in and picked up the goose. She didn't protest as he placed her in the pack. "I hope you can be quiet, please," he asked. I'm not ready to see the giant yet.

Jack arrived at the kitchen, and it was dark and cold. He climbed the counter by the sink and he noticed how much stronger he was than the last time he was here. He reached up into the cupboard and spoke to the harp.

"Hello there," he said. "My name is Jack." The harp looked at him suspiciously, and Jack grew nervous as he heard a few sounds start to come from the strings. Unlike the beautiful melody the harp played before, these sounds were discordant and growing louder. "Please don't do that!" He whispered. "I'm not here to steal you. I'm here to rescue you and return you to the church." The sounds faded and the harp's expression grew curious.

"I live in the village below. Many years ago, the giant stole you from the church and brought you here so he could keep your beautiful songs all to himself. I'm trying to bring you home." The harp looked impassive, and Jack wasn't sure what to do.

"If you want to stay," Jack offered, "I'll leave you here and won't touch you again. But if you want to go home, I need to place you in the backpack, and you have to be quiet." The most beautiful sound softly emerged from the harp, and Jack instantly thought of his father. He knew what the harp wanted, and he carefully placed her in the pack with the goose.

"Now I have to find the giant and get him to chase me," Jack said.

"He will kill you!" a high-pitched voice answered. Startled, Jack turned and saw a small bird resting in the window.

"I hope he doesn't kill me," Jack replied. "I'm trying to get him to follow me down the beanstalk and then I'll chop it down and kill him."

"You plan to kill the giant?" the little bird asked.

"Yes."

The bird shook its beak. "I don't think your chances are good, but I will help you. The giant is sleeping now. Soon he and the giantess will wake up and come to the kitchen to eat. Why don't you leave your hat on the floor so when the giant comes he will see that a human was here.

"Then after he realizes it, I can start squawking and getting his attention and make sure he sees you running down the road."

"That could work," Jack mused. "How do I know you won't betray me?"

"You don't," the bird replied. "But if I wanted to betray you, I could have done it already and the giant would already be here."

Jack laughed and for the first time that morning he felt hopeful. "You're right. I trust you. Where do you think I should go?"

"Walk down the road to the haystack and hide out of view. When you hear me squawking, it means I'm trying to get the giant to see you. Come out from the haystack and make sure the giant sees you then run for your life!"

Jack followed the plan. He could feel the weight of the goose and the harp in his pack, and they seemed lighter than the rocks he used to practice carrying them. He sat down behind the haystack and waited.

The giant yawned as he lumbered out of bed. "Hurry up," he shouted at the giantess. "You need to fix my breakfast," he grumbled as he made his way to the kitchen.

Yawning, he sat down at the table waiting for the giantess to feed him. As he sat, he noticed a peculiar odor. He sniffed several times.

"So, what's this?" asked the giantess as she picked Jack's hat off the floor.

"FEE-FI-FO-FUM! I smell the blood of a human man. Be he alive or be he dead, I'll grind his bones to make my bread," the giant shouted. "Do you think I'm making up stories now?" he yelled at the giantess. "Where is he!" The giant started opening cupboards and knocking things over in a vain effort to find Jack.

The bird started squawking. It squawked and it called as it flew around the room. "BE STILL!" the giant shouted as he swung at the bird. The bird kept squawking and flying toward the window.

"You fool," the giantess shouted. "The bird is trying to show you the man and there he is!" she said as she pointed out the window to Jack who was standing near the haystack.

The giant squinted out the window, "Don't call me a fool! When I kill him and eat him I won't share any of him with you."

"Go get him then, or you won't be eating any meat!" she yelled. But the giant didn't hear her because he was already chasing Jack.

As soon as he saw the giant running toward him, Jack ran as fast as he could. Though he had spent hours running in preparation for this chase, it felt different now. He knew if he stumbled or fell that the giant would kill and eat him. All the preparation he had done didn't prepare him for the fear he felt as he ran with every ounce of his strength toward the beanstalk.

When he reached it, he didn't look back. He knew it didn't matter. He either had enough time to live or he didn't and worrying about it now would only slow him down. Jack climbed down the beanstalk at a breakneck pace that almost killed him. He slipped and fell and slipped and fell and blistered his hands as he made his way to the ground with all the haste he could manage.

Finally, he broke through the clouds and could see his little home at the base of the beanstalk. He felt the beanstalk swaying above him and knew the weight of the giant's body was near. As Jack approached the ground, he could see his mother holding his father's axe.

"Hurry, mother," Jack yelled as his feet touched the ground. The beanstalk swayed like an angry reed in a storm and Jack knew he had no time to spare.

THWACK! Jack swung the axe as hard as he could. THWACK! THWACK! THWACK! The beanstalk started to sway.

"Hurry, Jack! HURRY! God help us! I can see the giant," cried his mother.

THWACK! THWACK! THWACK! The beanstalk swayed harder. Jack swung with all his might and a loud CRACK thundered through the sky as the beanstalk snapped and fell. Jack and his mother heard the giant screaming as he fell toward the ground and a giant shadow covered the pasture as the giant and the beanstalk crashed to the ground.

The sound of his fall echoed through the land as the screaming of the giant stopped. In the still pasture, they could see the form of the giant on the ground. "Here mother," Jack said handing her his pack. "There is a goose inside. I don't know if she is magic, but I rescued her. The harp is there too." Jack approached the giant. His mother started to follow, but Jack said, "Please, mother. Let me do this alone."

Jack carefully touched the giants face and reluctantly lifted the giant's eyelid with his axe. The giant was dead. There was no life in his eyes.

"Good job, young man," the old woman cackled. Standing beside him was the old woman who traded him the beans. She was holding his cow. "I'm going to give her back to you now. I've decided I don't need her, and I think she missed you."

"Thank you," Jack said quietly.

"You're welcome," she answered. "But don't ever forget, Jack, that this was always inside you. I only helped you find the path." And with that, she walked out of the pasture and down the road. To the end of his days, Jack never saw her again.

The next morning Jack went out to the goose and sitting beneath her was a golden egg, so he knew he and his mother wouldn't have to worry about money for the rest of their lives. Jack returned the harp to the church, and a spirit of love, kindness and peace came over all who heard her songs.

As the years passed, Jack was treated like a hero. He killed the giant, and he was a kind man. But the older he got, the more he knew that without his parents, the old woman who gave him the beans and the bird that helped him defeat the giant, he wouldn't have succeeded.

So, whenever anyone asked him how he killed the giant, he always said, "I was helped by my family, loved ones and friends. I could never have done it alone."

What can we learn from the story of *Jack and the Beanstalk*? Jack killed a giant. Or at least that's the story. Another way to look at it is that Jack was inspired with a plan of how a diminutive boy could physically prevail over a giant. Where did the inspiration to chop down the beanstalk come from? What if it hadn't worked? What if Jack's fears were so great that when he was inspired to chop down the beanstalk he thought: *Oh, well. I don't know. This plan, I mean it could work, but it probably won't. What if the beanstalk doesn't break? Or what if it does break and the giant falls and only breaks his arm? We would die! Maybe I shouldn't do it at all. I am only a boy, and he is a giant! Maybe my mother and I should just move and forget about our dreams…*

It is far more typical for us to destroy our own dreams and end our journeys before they begin than it is to follow them. Most of our courageous calls don't end in an epic battle between good and evil. Our calls to destiny don't always herald the beginning of a journey. Too often they die an ignoble death, unseen and unnoticed by anyone, sometimes not even ourselves.

The greatest enemy of courage is the negation of our life force by fear and feelings of doubt. It is difficult, if not impossible, to walk with a dragon when we are filled with doubt and fear. We can become almost paralyzed! The solution, the way to counter the doubt and fear is to be bold.

The story of *Jack and the Beanstalk* is filled with boldness. No matter the circumstance or his fears, Jack is always bold. It was bold (and probably a little foolish) to trade the cow for magic beans. It was bold to climb the beanstalk with no knowledge of what he would find. It was bold to go to the giant's castle instead of climbing down the beanstalk and returning home. It was bold to steal the harp, to craft a plan to kill the giant, and it was the epitome of boldness to put the plan into action and risk his life for the opportunity to kill the giant and avenge his father's death.

The way through the doubts and fears that will always arise in life is to be bold—not in a foolish way, but in wise and intuitively inspired ways. How do we know the difference? We learn from our mistakes, seek teachers to guide us and heed our dragons.

When we do that, our fears transform into hope and we are freed from the self-made prisons that bound us from discovering who we really are. We become free to answer our callings and take the journey that is the destiny and birthright of all human beings.

CHAPTER SIX

DISCERNMENT

Men who walk with dragons must practice discernment. They have to make choices and understand that choices have consequences. We must learn to discern wisely.

When we were children, we learned to make decisions by interpreting the circumstances around us and what the consequences of our choices would be. For example, if a parent or caregiver told us no and we did whatever we wanted to do anyway, there was often a punishment. We learned not to do it, or we learned that the punishment wasn't too bad so we did it anyway. Regardless of what we learned, that experience is the beginning of discernment.

It's difficult to practice discernment if we don't know what's right for us, what's important to us, where we want to go and how we might get there.

Life is filled with many decisions, and discernment—choosing where to put our energy, time, attention and efforts—is essential.

There is a story in Greek mythology of Tithonus, who was granted immortality, meaning he could never die.

What he discovered is that his choices, his decisions, his actions, no longer had any meaning once he was immortal. Tithonus went back to the Gods and asked to be relieved of immortality so he could live as a mortal again. He told the Gods he wanted mortality back so he could live a life that had meaning. The Gods wondered about this request, as they considered immortality one of their greatest gifts.

Eventually, they granted Tithonus' wish that his mortality be restored so he could age and die, and so his choices had meaning.

For an immortal, discernment isn't too important. Choices don't matter much if we can't die, because we can always make a different decision later. But we have the gift of mortality, and with that comes the need to discern what we do with our one "wild, precious life."

Discernment includes the ability to choose wisely. It allows us to grow from painful experiences and have a fuller, richer and more satisfying life. We learn to choose wisely by gaining an understanding of what is really important to us, what we are here to do, listening to our wise, inner voice and then courageously acting.

Every time we experience loss, pain and mortality as a natural consequence of a consciously discerned choice, there is an opportunity or a gift that comes with the pain we experience. These gifts are resources for living our destiny.

In the story of *The Frog Prince*, a princess learns that

discernment includes learning to see deeply and that first impressions aren't always true.

THE FROG PRINCE

Once upon a time, a king had three beautiful daughters. Although each of them stirred the hearts of their suitors, the youngest was the most beautiful of them all. Her eyes were deep brown, her figure perfectly formed, and her lips where full and sensuous. Her exquisite hands looked as if they had been crafted by a master sculptor. When she walked, it was with the grace of a swan.

Despite, or perhaps because of, her extraordinary beauty, she could be cruel. She knew everyone found her beautiful. Desirable. Eyes followed her wherever she went, and most who admired her couldn't avert their gaze quickly enough for the princess not to notice them longing after her.

As she approached womanhood and was considering whom she might marry, none of those who desired her seemed good enough. She liked to charm, but then would ignore those who craved her attentions.

She didn't have a bad heart. Part of her wanted to be loving and kind, but the influence of her extraordinary beauty had corrupted her thinking. She was vain and enjoyed holding power over those she enthralled.

She was accustomed to getting everything she wanted. Even her father, the king, wasn't good at telling her no.

Her sisters learned to tolerate her demands and forgive her selfishness by making excuses— "that is just the way she is."

The princess loved to wear beautiful things, and she preferred soft, smooth, silky clothing, intricate gold jewelry and anything opulent.

Her favorite possession was a polished gold ball. Her father had it made for her fourteenth birthday, and the servants polished it every night. She loved admiring her face in the reflective gold sphere, and she carried it everywhere. She constantly ran her fingers across the smooth, round surface and took great pride in believing that her bauble was the most beautiful possession in the kingdom.

Near the castle, stately old trees surrounded a deep pool fed by a waterfall. Some of the young men liked to jump from the edge of the waterfall into the pool, but none of them had ever touched the bottom.

The princess liked to sit in the shade of the trees and listen to the water tumbling into the pool. As she sat, she liked to play with her golden ball, tossing it, caressing it, and watching it gleam in the sun as it reflected the trees, the water and her countenance.

One afternoon as she sat in the shade listening to the water and playing with her golden ball, a large dog charged and started barking. "Go away!" she shouted. And though the dog ran off, she was so startled that she dropped her golden ball. It slowly rolled downward toward the pool and, though she tried to stop it, the ball slipped into the water and disappeared.

"My ball!" she cried. "My ball!" She placed her hand into the cool, flowing water but all that emerged was her wet arm. "I must have my ball," she wailed. As the finality of her loss grew in her mind, she became inconsolable. "My ball, my ball. I'd do anything to have my ball back."

"Princess, why are you so distraught?" an odd croaking voice asked. She looked around, but she was alone except for a frog who was slowly coming toward her out of the water. "What happened to cause you such pain?" the voice, which she could now see emanated from the frog, asked.

"I lost my ball," she stammered. "I need it back, and there is no way for me to get it. It rolled away from me and fell into the pool. It's gone forever," she started to cry.

"Don't worry, princess. I can help you," the frog offered.

"Would you? Would you please? I'd do anything for you if you can get my ball."

"I don't need many things..."

"I can give you jewels, gold, any of my clothes or even my crown!" she interrupted.

"No, no. I want for none of that. What I need, dear princess, is a companion. Someone to love me. All I ask is that every evening you let me sit with you at your table, eat with you from your plate, drink with you from your cup, and sleep with you in your bed."

"Of course, of course! If you can bring me my golden

ball, I promise I will do everything you ask."

"Wait here," the frog said as he hopped to the pool and disappeared. A quarter hour passed. *Where is that frog?* the princess wondered. *I don't think he knows how to get my ball back. The ugly creature probably swam away so as to not have to tell me he couldn't succeed.* But soon, as the princess watched the pool, she noticed a ripple moving toward the land's edge. A glint of gold broke the water's surface, and her heart leaped with joy.

"My ball! My ball!" she shouted as she reached into the water and grabbed it. The frog was so tired he could barely make his way onto the shore.

"I got it for you, my princess," he tiredly croaked. But, as he pulled himself out of the pool, she had already started running back to the castle. "Wait! Wait!" he called. "You promised to take me with you." Whether she couldn't hear him, forgot about him, or broke her promise to him, he didn't know. All he knew was that the princess was gone.

That evening, as the sun was setting and the royal family was sitting down to their evening meal, there came a strange sound from the castle door. "What is that odd noise?" the king asked. The youngest princess felt a stab of fear as she remembered her promise to the ugly frog. "It sounds as if someone is speaking," the king said. They all heard a voice chant:

Youngest king's daughter,
Let me come in,
I need what was promised,
Don't forget that we're friends!

"I'll get it, Father," she said. Her sisters exchanged suspicious looks, as it wasn't like the youngest princess to volunteer to do any work.

She opened the door and below her knees was the frog who rescued her gold ball. "Go away!" she hissed. "You're an ugly frog, and if you leave now I'll come to the pool tomorrow and bring you some food and a pretty gold ring." Without waiting for an answer, she shut the door and returned to the table.

"What was that, my daughter?" the king asked.

"Nothing, Father. It was only an annoying frog."

"What does he want with you?"

"He—well…" she stammered, "…he rescued the golden ball you gave me from the pool, and he expects a reward."

"That is a great favor. What is he asking for?" the queen asked.

"Oh, it's stupid. I offered him food and gold, but the silly frog wants to sit with me at the table, eat with me from my plate, drink with me from my cup and sleep with me in my bed. Can you believe that?"

"Why would he ask these things?" the king asked.

The young princess grew quiet. Though she was vain and self-absorbed, she didn't want to lie to her father. "The frog recovered my golden ball under the condition that I become his companion, and I said I would, but I never thought he would really come to the castle. I mean, how can I, a beautiful princess, make an ugly frog like him my companion?"

Again they hear the sound at the door:

Youngest king's daughter,

Let me come in,

I need what was promised,

Don't forget that we're friends!

"Father! Make him go away! I don't ever want to see that ugly frog again."

"I'm sorry my dear, but that which you have promised him you must do. Go now to the door, and bring this frog here to the table so you may keep the promise you have made."

With her eyes welling up with tears, the young princess went to the door and, when she returned, hopping behind her was the frog. As she sat down, he called, "Pick me up so I may eat from your plate." She reached down and grabbed the slimy creature and placed him next to her plate. He ate a few bites and said, "Princess, I'm thirsty. Please lift me to your cup so I might quench my thirst." The princess looked as if she would cry, but the steely gaze of the king was upon her. She lifted the frog to the edge of her cup and tipped it so he could drink his fill.

"That was very fine. Thank you. Would you like to eat some more now?"

"No! I'm no longer hungry." Everyone could see she was upset and would not eat or drink after the frog.

"Very well then, princess. I think it's time we went to bed."

The princess looked imploringly at the king. But,

rather than free her from the frog's request, he said, "Good night, my daughter. I hope you and your frog companion sleep well." Pursing her lips and glaring at her father, the princess tucked the frog in the crook of her arm and carried him with her to her bedchamber.

She shut her door, dropped him roughly to the floor, undressed and climbed into her bed. A fishy smell disturbed her, and she realized the frog had hopped onto her pillow! He was staring at her with his ugly, beady eyes, but before she could yell at him to leave her bed, he said, "Good night, sweet princess. Sleep well, and may the dreams of the angels guide and protect you this and every night."

It was such a nice blessing she didn't have the will to yell at him, so she turned her head away so as not to see or smell him, and she fell asleep.

The next morning when she awoke, the frog was gone. *Thank goodness* she thought. *I am glad that's over and done with.* But that evening as the family sat down to dinner, they heard the now familiar call:

Youngest king's daughter
Let me come in,
I need what was promised,
Don't forget that we're friends!

"I'll go let him in," she sighed. She returned with the frog, whom she placed on the table. He ate from her plate and drank from her cup. When they were finished, the frog went with her to her bedroom.

"Princess, thank you," the frog said.

"Thank you for what?" she asked.

"For keeping your word with me, and letting me sleep in your bed and eat from your plate and drink from your cup."

"It's what I promised. I have no choice," she said flatly.

"That's not true," said the frog. "It is what you promised, but many people promise many things. That doesn't mean they always keep their promises. You have a choice, and you are choosing to keep your promise to me even though I am an ugly, stinky frog and you are the most beautiful princess in the kingdom."

"How would you know I am beautiful?" the princess asked.

"I may be a frog, but I'm not blind. I know I am a fortunate frog to be so close to you."

Despite his ugliness, the princess was moved. "You feel fortunate to be with me?" she asked.

"Yes, but I feel most fortunate that you didn't betray me."

"I almost did!" she admitted.

"But you didn't. Here I am in the silken bed of a beautiful princess with a full stomach and quenched thirst. I think it makes me the most fortunate frog alive. Good night, sweet princess. Sleep well, and may the dreams of the angels guide and protect you this and every night." And then the frog lightly croaked as he quickly fell asleep.

The princess lay awake listening to the light sounds

of the sleeping frog but also thinking about what he said. She realized she could have disobeyed her father. He would have been angry, but he always forgave her. Or she could have taken the frog to her room and smashed him with her boots. But she didn't. She realized that because she had made a promise to the frog, as unpleasant as it was to keep, it was better to do that than to break her word.

The next morning the frog was gone, and for a moment the princess almost missed him.

That evening as the royal family gathered for dinner they heard the frog call:

Youngest king's daughter,
Let me come in,
I need what was promised,
Don't forget that we're friends!

"I'll go get him," the princess said as she left the table and brought the frog back with her. Without any prompting, she set him next to her plate, and when he ate his fill, she even took a bite after him. When he finished drinking, she took a small sip from her cup. And when they went to bed together, she placed him on her pillow.

Neither of them said anything. Finally, when the silence became too much, the princess quietly said, "Good night, frog."

"Good night, sweet princess. Sleep well, and may the dreams of the angels guide and protect you this and every night."

"Good night, frog," she whispered a few minutes

later, and she turned and gave him a quick kiss. The frog twitched, but whether he was awake and knew she kissed him, or asleep and dreaming, the princess couldn't tell.

Her dreams that night were delightful. She imagined that she finally met the love of her life. Her deepest fear had always been that her inside could never be as beautiful as her outside, and that if anyone really got to know her that eventually they would be disappointed.

She woke as the morning sun slipped past the drawn curtains and lit her room. *I must still be dreaming,* she thought, as she could still feel the arms of a beautiful young man she dreamt about wrapped around her. Turning over she saw the most handsome young man she had ever seen. His skin was smooth, his hair dark and full, and in sleep he looked more like an angel than a man. As she stared at him, he opened his eyes.

"Princess?" he asked, "Is it really over? Am I here in your bed with you?"

"Over? Who are you? And what do you mean?"

The young man sat up and looked at his hands, rubbed his legs and arms, and grinned at her. "It is over! You've done it! You've saved me!" and he grabbed her in a tight embrace. She knew she should feel frightened that a stranger, no matter how handsome, was holding her tightly in her own bed. But she felt safe, secure and loved.

"Who are you?" she asked again.

"Don't you know, princess?" he asked with a twinkle in his eye.

"No," she shook her head. "I feel like I should know you, or be angry with you for being in my bed, but I feel none of those things."

"You invited me to your bed," he said. "You also let me eat from your plate and drink from your cup."

A chill ran down her spine and her body quivered, "You! You… are the frog?"

He nodded. "I was captured by someone evil who turned me into a frog. They told me the only way the spell could ever be broken is if a young woman would take me, an ugly frog, as her companion to sit with her at her table, eat with her from her plate, drink with her from her cup and sleep with her in her bed and finally kiss me because she loved me. You have done that dear, beautiful princess. The spell is broken and you have set me free. Thank you for keeping your word to me and for kissing me."

"You know I kissed you?" she asked.

He nodded slyly. "I wasn't asleep. I'm not asleep now either," and he pulled her closer to him and kissed her.

Later that morning, a carriage pulled by eight white horses came to the castle, and the young princess discovered that the handsome young man was a prince. His servant, Henry, had been faithfully searching for him, and with her father's permission and blessing, the young princess left with the prince to meet his father and see the prince reunited with those he loved.

As they galloped away from her home, a loud cracking sound startled her. "What's breaking?" the princess asked.

"Don't worry your highness," Henry said. "When the prince was stolen I was so distraught that I had my heart bound with three iron bands to keep it from breaking. What you are hearing are the bands breaking and setting my heart free again."

The young princess realized how much Henry loved the young prince, and she understood that the handsome young man who had been a frog was loved by many. She felt grateful that they had been brought together.

The prince and princess were married and eventually had children of their own. When the prince's father died, the prince became king and the princess became queen, but neither of them ever forgot the memory of their courtship. Every so often, the queen would say, "Your Frogness...I mean Your Highness," and the king and queen would give a private smile to each other as they remembered the good fortune of how they were brought together.

*
* *

As we can see in the story of *The Frog Prince*, the gift of discernment works when it is practiced. We ignore it our peril. When we take the time to heed and practice it, it works. But if we allow inflations, infatuations and enthrallments to steal the gift of discernment from us, we can't avoid the consequences.

A powerful resource to practicing discernment is personal integrity. Recognizing that we are making the choices for our own life and that it is our responsibility to make the best choices we can, is our first and foremost ally in choosing wisely.

The princess practiced integrity and honored the promise she made to the frog, even though at first she didn't want to keep it. Because she chose wisely, listened to her father, and kept her word to the frog, she eventually discovered what she didn't expect to happen: that she loved the frog despite his appearance.

To walk with dragons, we must make our choices wisely. To choose wisely requires wisdom and an awareness and insight sometimes deeper than that we usually employ. This is where discovering our calling, using our intuition and having courage can all help us be wise.

When we practice discernment, miracles can happen. Frogs can turn into princes, old grudges can mend, and relationships we thought were lost can be healed.

Few decisions are more difficult than having to discern when it is time to let something live or die, or whether we should keep something or let it go. Most of us have let certain friendships or relationships last longer than we knew was wise, but it can be hard to let what we are familiar with die. It is almost impossible to let something go unless we have faith that in the process of letting something die, we make room for new life to appear again. Conversely, when we keep something alive after we know it is time to let it go, we prevent anything new from appearing in our lives.

Before the princess met the frog, her vision of a companion was someone beautiful and comparable in stature to her. If she hadn't been willing to let that belief go, she would never have experienced the open-mindedness necessary to let her relationship with the frog unfold, and she never would have discovered the frog was truly a prince.

So many choices and decisions in life are challenging. Our conscious mind isn't sufficient to fully make many of life's most important decisions. When we are aware that decisions we make will have significant consequences, we can easily feel anxious and afraid, which only makes our conscious mind's ability to make a wise decision more difficult. Our capacity for wise conscious decision making is diminished when we are stressed, anxious, angry or afraid.

It is especially in these times that practicing discernment and choosing wisely will help us navigate the challenges we face. As the princess demonstrates in this story, one of the ways we can choose wisely is to act with integrity and be true to our word. Dragons are drawn to integrity, loyalty and bravery, and they will help us choose wisely if we allow them to do so.

CHAPTER SEVEN

INTEGRITY

There are many definitions of integrity. Some define integrity as being integrated or whole. I like to think of developing integrity as like a dull stone coming out polished from a rock tumbler; we become whole with our rough spots rubbed off from our encounters with life.

A building or structure has integrity if it is solid and well built. There is a story told that in the time of the Greeks that craftsmen who worked in stone and marble would sometimes fill in nicks and scrapes on the surface of the stone with wax to conceal imperfections. When a stone had no wax hiding flaws it was "sincere" (from Latin, *sin*: without, and *cera*: wax). A person, idea or thing that is sincere has integrity.

To have integrity in our lives requires an understanding and consideration of spiritual principles. It includes asking or knowing: What is our calling? Who or what do we serve?

How we manifest spiritual principles in our lives are our values. For example, honesty is a spiritual principle. How we practice honesty in our lives is a value. Spiritual principles don't change, but our values, and the way we integrate those principles in our lives, evolve throughout our lifetime.

The gap between the precepts we choose in how we live our lives (our values) and timeless spiritual principles, is where much of our opportunity for development and growth resides.

For example, if we want to be an honest person but we often engage in small dishonest acts at school or work, the gap between the spiritual principle of honesty and the values we create for ourselves of what it means to live honestly is our opportunity for growth.

For some, cheating on a test at school or stealing small office supplies at work is consistent with their values and they can "live with it." For others, doing that is a violation of their integrity and to do so creates an opportunity for further dishonesty to enter their lives.

Spiritual principles are usually easier to understand than values. They are universal and transcend societies and cultures. Values require reflection, effort and action. They evolve and change. Creating personal values requires deeply knowing ourselves and integrating our values with spiritual principles, our calling and destiny.

To walk with a dragon requires integrity. It means the consideration, integration and application of spiritual principles as values in our life. If our values are faulty, meaning they aren't congruent with spiritual principles and our calling, they won't be sufficient to guide us.

Some of the greatest heroes made spiritual principles

like duty, loyalty, courage, honor and kindness the foundation of their values. To live our calling means we can't take shortcuts. There is no "quick fix" to creating integrity in our lives.

When we live a life of mature values, values that are right for us and congruent with our calling and destiny, we cannot fail. We cannot really "die." If we believe a coward dies a thousand deaths and a hero only one, a life built on values never dies. We could be martyred, we may not physically take every step we hoped to take, our time on this planet may end sooner than we or our loved ones hoped—but a life lived by values based on spiritual principles always endures.

Integrity is the consistent application of spiritual principles in all areas of life. No matter the circumstances, no matter who hurt us, no matter what excuse we might make up to violate them. It means always doing the right things for us, because it's the right thing for us. Especially when no one is watching.

In the story of *The Three little Pigs*, there is an affection and loyalty between them. But they aren't all in the same place in the development of their values.

This isn't so much a problem as it is a fact. It's simply where each of them are in their personal growth. What can be a problem are the consequences caused from not doing the work necessary to form values that create a mature, responsible and principle-based life.

While we are free to choose our actions, we are almost

never free to choose the consequences of those actions. Consequences of our actions are outside our control. When we take actions before we develop values based on spiritual principles, the consequences can be disastrous.

Heroes aren't impulsive, though they sometimes act quickly. Their actions rest on the bedrock of their values, which rests upon a foundation of spiritual principles. Heroes have integrity, and that integrity is a large part of what defines who they are.

To be heroic doesn't always appear extraordinary. Sometimes the most heroic things we do can appear ordinary and mundane. Heroism includes going to work to take care of our families while suffering from a life-threatening disease, working two part-time jobs after school to help our parents pay the rent, or comforting others when we are in pain ourselves. As we see in *The Three Little Pigs*, seemingly ordinary actions can have extraordinary consequences.

THE THREE LITTLE PIGS

Once upon a time, there were three little pigs. They were young, but not children, and at the time in their lives that they needed to live on their own.

Although all three had good hearts and were kind, the oldest pig was lazy. He preferred laying in the sunshine and eating more than he liked gathering food. The youngest liked to tumble, play and swim. He didn't like to do anything very long. "The sooner the better" was his motto. He always wanted to try something new.

The middle pig liked to lay in the sunshine and eat with the oldest pig, and he enjoying playing and swimming with the youngest pig. But he had a dream of living in a comfortable home where his friends and family could visit him and where he would feel safe on dark, scary nights.

One day a farmer drove past the three pigs in a cart overflowing with straw. "This is my chance," the oldest pig said. "I can make my house of straw and, when I am really hungry, I will have something to eat!"

"Hello, Mr. Farmer," the oldest pig shouted. "Where are you going with all the straw?"

"I've got more than I need," the farmer said. "I'm giving this load away to anyone who wants it." The farmer squinted at the pig. "Could you use this straw? I'd be happy to unload it here and return to my farm."

The oldest pig happily took the farmer's straw. With the help of the two younger pigs, he quickly built a house of straw. It wasn't too sturdy, light appeared between the cracks, and the roof wouldn't keep out all the rain, but it did protect him from the sun.

"What a lovely house!" he said, as he grabbed a piece of straw and nibbled it. "It's good to eat too!"

The next day, a woodman drove a cart filled with twigs past the three pigs. The youngest pig shouted, "Hey, Mr. Woodman! What are you doing with all those twigs?"

"Building a bonfire," he shrugged. "Got no other use for it. Would you like to have some?"

"I'd like to have them all," he said as he quickly unloaded the cart. "Now I can have a house too. The branches are small, and we can build it quickly!" he said to the two older pigs, for he never liked to do anything very long or by himself.

The older pigs helped him, and by evening a twig house for the youngest pig stood not far from the straw house of the oldest pig.

On the third day, a mason came driving a cart of bricks past the three pigs. The cart moved slowly as his horse struggled to pull the weight. "Hello, Mr. Mason," the middle pig called. "You have quite a load of bricks. I hope you don't have too far to go."

"Sadly I must go a long way," he sighed. "I was building a home and had too many bricks. I don't want to abandon them, but I don't know if my old horse can pull them all the way back to my shop."

"Would you like to sell them?" the pig politely asked.

"What would you do with them?" the mason asked curiously.

"I want to build a home that can stand the push of the wind, the fall of the rain and keep me safe and warm at night."

The mason nodded. "That seems a wise thing, Master Pig, but it isn't easy to lay bricks. You must put mortar between them, set them carefully, and wait for them to cure before setting more above them. Can you do that?"

"I think I can if you teach me. I am willing to learn."

"All right then," the mason laughed. "You may have these bricks, and I'll show you the basics of using a trowel to set your bricks properly."

The pig was a good student because he wanted to learn. He listened carefully and followed the mason's example. Together, they unloaded the bricks and the pig started to prepare a foundation as the mason taught him to do.

"Come help me," the pig called to the younger and older pig. "I want to build a house too."

"That's too much work," the older pig complained.

"It's sunny, and I'm hot and want to swim," the younger pig protested.

"Please, can't you help me?" the middle pig pleaded. The older and younger pigs shook their snouts and left him alone. He felt scared. There were so many bricks and each one was heavy. He hadn't built a house of bricks before, and trying to do it alone was hard.

He thought about forgetting the whole thing. *Maybe the walls will collapse* he fretted. *After all, I know nothing about building a brick house.* He looked at the older pig's house of straw as it reflected brightly in the afternoon sun. The younger pig's house of twigs looked comfortable too. *Why must my home be so difficult?* He wondered. *How can I build my home with no one to help me?*

Not knowing what to do, and feeling overwhelmed and alone, he ate a small meal, drank a glass of water and looked back at the pile of the bricks the mason had left him.

The mason believed I could do it he thought. *He wouldn't have given me the bricks and taught me what to do unless he believed in me. Maybe I could start with one row for the foundation and perhaps a little bit at a time I can start to build my house.*

He laid the bricks and carefully placed the mortar as the mason taught him. It looked good. When he finished the first row and stood back, it seemed solid and true. The pig was pleased with his work. Hope filled his heart as he started to believe he could do this.

The next day, the other pigs still didn't help him. The pile of bricks and the task ahead still overwhelmed him, but he continued to place one brick at a time. Soon the walls of his home were a few feet tall. The door was a challenge, but he kept working. The more he worked, the better he became at his craft. By the time he was mounting his chimney on the roof, he felt confident. He had learned how to lay bricks, and his house was solid.

"What a beautiful house," the older pig exclaimed. He could see the middle pig's home was nicer than his." Sorry I didn't help," the older pig said. "But I'm really not very useful at hard work."

"You did a nice job," the younger pig said a little guiltily. "I'm sorry I didn't help either. The weather was so nice, but if you like I can help a little now."

"It's mostly done," the middle pig laughed. Although he was disappointed they didn't help him, he was glad that they weren't avoiding him anymore.

The next day as the morning sun shone bright in the sky and the oldest pig slept soundly in his house of straw, there came a loud rap on his door.

"Hello," he cried groggily. "Who is it?"

"Little pig, little pig, let me come in," a voice commanded. Opening his eyes and peering through the straw he saw a big, bad wolf!

"Not by the hair of my chinny chin chin," he squealed.

"Then I'll huff, and I'll puff and I'll blow your house in!" the big, bad wolf roared. There was a loud sound of rushing air and the older pig squealed in fright as the wolf began to blow his house down. As the straw walls collapsed and his house fell down around him, the oldest pig ran as fast as he could to the youngest pig's house of sticks.

"Let me in!" he yelled. The younger pig opened the door and stared at the frightened pig.

"What's wrong?" he asked.

"SHUT THE DOOR!" he shouted. "My house was destroyed by a big, bad wolf, and I barely escaped with my life!"

"Here, sit down," the youngest pig said, trying to keep the older pig calm.

KNOCK! KNOCK! KNOCK! Came a loud sound from the door. "Don't answer," the frightened oldest pig whimpered.

"There's no one here! Go away!" the youngest pig squealed.

"Little pig, little pig, let me come in," said the big, bad wolf.

The two pigs stared at each other, and the oldest pig shook his head no.

"Not by the hair of my chinny chin chin," answered the youngest pig.

"Then I'll huff and I'll puff and I'll blow your house in," roared the wolf. The youngest pig heard a loud sound of rushing air, and the walls of his twig house started to wobble and shake.

"It's going to collapse," cried the oldest pig. "Hurry! The brick house is our only hope!" As the twigs collapsed and the door crashed in, the two pigs ran as fast as they could to the brick house.

Fortunately, the door was open, and they slammed it shut as they ran inside.

"What's going on?" the middle pig asked as he looked curiously at the frightened older and younger pigs who were both gasping for breath.

"Our houses are destroyed," they wailed. "A big, bad wolf came and destroyed them and tried to eat us! I think he is going to come here next."

No sooner did they warn the middle pig than came a loud rap at the door. KNOCK! KNOCK! KNOCK! "Little pig, little pig, let me come in," shouted the wolf.

Standing bravely by the door the middle pig said, "Not by the hair of my chinny chin chin."

"Then I'll huff and I'll puff and I'll blow your house in."

The older and younger pigs cowered in a corner as they heard the familiar sound of rushing air. But when the big, bad wolf tried to blow down the house of brick, it stood strong. The wolf paced outside and tried blowing all of the walls, but the wolf's efforts were in vain.

"Your house is so strong," said the older pig.

"Thank you for letting us in," said the younger pig.

"Do you hear something?" asked the middle pig. The two other pigs listened closely, and all of them heard the sound of paws scurrying across the roof. "He's going to try to come down the chimney," whispered the middle pig.

A warm fire blazed in the brick fireplace. The middle pig pointed to a giant iron pot, and with the help of the older and younger pigs placed it in the fireplace. Soon the paws of the wolf descended from the chimney to the fireplace, but the pot was so large that the wolf thought he was in the house. The moment they saw the hair of his head go into the pot the middle pig shouted, "Now!" The three little pigs slid the lid over the pot and the big, bad wolf howled as he was trapped inside.

"Let me out! Let me out!" he pleaded. "If you let me out, I'll never hurt you again!" But the three little pigs were wise and did not trust him, and they left the lid on the pot until all the sounds ceased. When they pulled the pot from the fire, all that remained inside was a large pile of greasy, gray ash.

The three pigs looked at each other. "Thank you," the older pig said. "I'm sorry I was lazy and didn't help you."

"I'm sorry too," the younger pig added. "I should have helped you build your house instead of playing in the sun and swimming."

"I'm glad you are here with me now, and next time I think things will be different." He smiled at them. It warmed his heart that, because he built his home of bricks, the big, bad wolf couldn't eat any of them.

The three little pigs stepped outside and began to play together. They swam, lay in the sun and frolicked in the grass. And although they looked like they did before the big, bad wolf came to eat them, each of them was now a little wiser.

*
* *

When thinking about the story of *The Three Little Pigs*, we usually realize that most of us share aspects of all three. Sometimes we are the youngest pig who wants to play. Other times we are the oldest pig who is lazy and wants things to come easily. And sometimes we are industrious and wise.

The middle pig developed a sense of integrity that his two companions lacked. Fortunately, his foresight, wisdom and effort saved all of their lives.

If his house had lacked integrity—if it wasn't "sincere"—the big, bad wolf would have eaten all three of them. While they would have learned a valuable lesson, they would have died!

One way to practice integrity is to aspire to have integrity in everything we do. When we are impeccable with our word, brave in our actions, kind in our deeds and loving to all, there is little we can't accomplish.

The challenge is that none of us always do these things perfectly. To err is human, it seems to be our birthright and fate. Wisdom means quickly correcting our actions when we make a mistake, and not letting our past errors determine our present behaviors.

We always have this moment, the one we are living in now, to act with integrity. The most valuable integrity is the kind we practice right now. Today. While it can be hard, the reward is well worth the effort. Dragons are drawn to integrity, courage, self-discipline, loyalty and bravery. Fortune favors the bold and, when we act with integrity, our lives support us to live our calling accompanied by our dragons.

Chapter Eight

WISDOM

To find our unique personal quest requires a sense of our destiny, full engagement of our sense of intuition, discernment in the choices we must make, courage to face and accept our calling and integrity to our highest self. It also requires wisdom.

While wisdom is a fruit that comes from the pursuit of other principles and resources, it is also a gift or grace that comes to those who act wisely. The paradox of wisdom is that the more one practices and heeds it in daily life, the greater the influence it has over us. Its voice grows louder as we practice the habit of listening to it.

Conversely, the more wisdom is ignored, the less influence it bestows and the greater the folly of our choices and actions.

The personal evolution of wisdom requires discernment, integrity, knowing who we really are, a connection to that which is greater and a willingness to grow, learn and heal.

There is a story told by Rumi, the Persian poet, that describes the paramount importance of having wisdom about our calling.

"There is one thing above all other things in this world that you must never forget is yours to do. Should you forget all other things in life but not this one, you need not worry at all.

But if you do everything else in life and forget this one thing, it is as if you have done nothing in your life.

It is like a great ruler sent you to some faraway land to do one essential task, and you do hundreds of other tasks, but you do not complete the one task you were sent to do. So it is with all of us, that we come to this world to do that task which is ours personally to do. That work is our purpose and it is unique to each person. If you do not do this one task, it is as if a knife of the finest steel were fastened to a wall to hang things on, when a nail could have replaced the knife for that simple purpose.

Remember in the deepest places of your being the presence of your Lord. Give all your life and effort to the one who already owns your breath and moments. If you don't do this, you will be like the one who takes a precious dagger and mounts it on his wall for a peg when any nail could have easily sufficed. If you don't do this one task, you will be squandering that which is most unique and special about you and ignoring your dignity and your purpose."

One of the greatest roles of any parent is to try to encourage the development of wisdom in their children. Good fathers and mothers try to teach their sons and daughters the ways of the world, and how to avoid mistakes.

Teaching children requires wisdom from the parent,

but no matter how wise the parent is, the child still has free will and the ability to embrace or reject the parent's teachings.

Fortunately, most often when sons or daughters ignore their parent's wise counsel, the price isn't too high and the scars aren't too deep. There are times, however, when failing to heed the wisdom of a parent can cost a child deeply. It can even cost them their life.

This dynamic between parent and child, teacher and student, mentor and acolyte is as old as humankind. It is the curse and blessing of every parent, mentor and teacher to take joy when their wisdom is heeded, and grieve when it is ignored. Sometimes the grief feels so intense that it is almost impossible to keep going, to get up one more day and face life on its own terms.

Another gift of wisdom, even in the face of feelings that may seem like they will kill us, is the awareness that feelings will pass and, as long as we are alive, the world is worth waking up for.

Soon enough, life will end for all of us. Few lessons are more obvious then realizing life is short, and spending time with people we love is wise.

Wisdom teaches us that life continues here regardless of whether we are still alive, and that this life is for the living. It is meant to be lived reflectively and prospectively, not mired in the nostalgic regrets of what might have been, or mourning our inevitable and painful losses. The promise of hope that is enshrouded by wisdom is that no matter what befalls us, there is always a wise path through every challenge.

In the story of Icarus and Daedalus, a father experiences the tragedy all parent's fear, and his life is forever changed.

ICARUS AND DAEDALUS

Once upon a time, many centuries ago on the island of Crete, there lived a man named Daedalus and his young son Icarus. Daedalus was a devoted father and an inventor of wonderful mechanical creations.

Daedalus was so talented that he attracted the attention of the king. When a princess was born to King Minos, Daedalus created a tiny mechanical bird that chirped when the sun rose.

King Minos recognized that Daedalus had an extraordinary gift. But rather than having him make more beautiful things, the king asked him if he might be able to invent something that would give him more power. A few months later, Daedalus presented plans for a giant labyrinth to hold a prisoner: a half-man and half-bull monster known as the Minotaur.

The king was pleased. Unfortunately, he was also greedy. He wanted Daedalus to serve only him, so he had his royal guards take Daedalus and his young son Icarus and lock them away in a cave high above the sea. The king wanted to make sure that only he could benefit from Daedalus' extraordinary creations. The only entrances to the cave were through the labyrinth containing the Minotaur, which was guarded by the King's soldiers, and an entrance overlooking the sea high up on the side of a cliff.

At first, Daedalus didn't mind his imprisonment. King Minos provided everything Daedalus requested without question. They had food, drink, tools of all shapes, rare metals, leather, parchment and candles to work late into the night. Daedalus lived happily for years working away on an endless variety of wondrous inventions. And young Icarus, although sometimes bored, was usually quite happy helping out his father and playing with the mechanical toys Daedalus made for him.

When Icarus became a teenager, Daedalus began to worry that being locked away was not good for his son. Icarus grew tired of the cold, damp cave. He complained he had no life of his own, and he wanted to see and experience the world beyond the cave.

On his fifteenth birthday Icarus broke into a rage, "Father! I want an adventure! I want to meet a girl and someday have a child of my own! I can't ask a wife to come live with you and me in this cave. I hate it here!" He shouted. "I hate the King and I hate you!"

Even though Icarus apologized the next day for his hurtful words, Daedalus knew that Icarus needed to leave the cave and go back into the world.

The next time King Minos visited, Daedalus said, "Your Majesty, Icarus is becoming a young man. Could you please allow him to join your royal guard and seek a life in your service while I continue to make things for you?"

The King stared at Daedalus and finally said, "I shall consider your request. Now, please, show me your idea for giant mechanical soldiers."

The king didn't want to let Icarus go. He believed that Icarus might have his father's talents and know his secrets, as Icarus had watched and learned from his father for his entire life. He did not want to risk anyone else getting access to the mechanical wonders Daedalus created and that Icarus might someday produce.

A few weeks later, King Minos returned to Daedalus and said, "I have thought about your suggestion that Icarus enter my service, but Icarus provides the greatest service to me by keeping you company here."

"But, sire…" interrupted Daedalus.

"Enough!" ordered King Minos, "My decision is made. Icarus shall remain in the cave with you."

After the king left, Daedalus turned to Icarus to explain that there was nothing more he could do, but when he saw the look of utter despair on his son's face, Daedalus' heart broke. He vowed that he would make his son free.

Daedalus stood at the entrance of the cave overlooking the sea, watching the waves crash on the rocks below and the seagulls circle over the cliffs. It was spring and the nests on the cliffs were filled with eggs and chicks.

Icarus walked up beside his father and said softly, "How I envy those baby birds, for soon their wings will be strong and they'll be able to fly away from this wretched cliff."

Daedalus blinked, a smile slowly growing on his face. He turned to Icarus, his eyes twinkling, "Well then, my son, we'd best start working on strengthening your wings so you can be off with the others!"

Daedalus used strips of leather and fine twigs to fashion a broom and a large net, which Icarus used to dangle down toward the cliffs to sweep up the feathers near the seagull nests. For many weeks, Icarus carefully gathered every feather he could reach.

While Icarus gathered feathers, Daedalus created thin tubes of light metal that he used to form the frame of two pairs of man-sized wings. He used leather strips to create a harness and pulleys to allow the wearer to flap and tilt the wings in various directions. Then he took the feathers that Icarus had collected and used candle wax to begin to attach the feathers to the light metal frames.

"Two frames?" Icarus asked his father, "Are you coming too?"

Daedalus clasped his son on the shoulder and replied, "I am, my son. Thank you for reminding me that of all my creations, you are the most important to me. I'm sorry that it's taken me so long to free us both."

It was painstaking work collecting the feathers and attaching them one by one to the frames but many weeks later, Daedalus declared the wings complete.

The morning they were to leave, Daedalus reminded

Icarus one last time, "Remember, you must be cautious when we fly. If you fly too close to the ocean, your wings will become too heavy with the water that sprays off the waves, but if you fly too close to the sun, the wax will melt and you will lose feathers. Follow my path closely and you'll be fine."

Icarus nodded, "Of course, Father. I will. I'll follow your path the whole time," and he excitedly slid his arms into the harness. He half-listened as his father explained how to open the wings wide to catch the air currents and how to use the pulleys to steer. He was so enthralled with the idea of leaving the cave and flying, he didn't pay close attention to his father's words. He merely nodded in agreement as his mind savored the thought of leaving the cave, flying and meeting a girl.

After an eager hug for good luck, Daedalus and Icarus stepped into the entrance of the cave overlooking the sea, spread their wings as wide as they would go and leaped, one after the other, out over the ocean.

The wind caught Icarus' wings almost immediately, and up he soared. Icarus threw his head back and laughed as the startled seagulls dodged away from him and then swooped back squawking warnings when he steered too close to the nesting cliffs.

Daedalus shouted to his son to be careful, and to stop playing with the birds and follow him toward the shore of an island in the distance. But Icarus was having too much fun. Instead of listening to his father, Icarus indulged in his sudden freedom and ignored everything his father told him.

Daedalus grew afraid as he saw Icarus take bigger and greater risks. He knew that the wings he created for his son had strict limits, and that Icarus would crash if he didn't heed his advice.

Icarus flew away from his father, so he wouldn't have to hear him shouting at him to be careful. He watched the seagulls rise on the air currents high over the sea and decided he wanted to fly like they did. He followed the seagulls up and up, higher into the sky.

"No, Icarus! Stop!" shouted Daedalus, "The wax will melt if it gets too warm. Not so high. Not so high!"

But Icarus was too far away to hear his father's warnings. He loved the warmth of the sun and the rush of the air as it swept back his hair and blew over his body. He grew bolder and flew higher still. All of a sudden, he began to feel wax dripping down his arms and he saw feathers were falling like snowflakes down around him.

His excitement at the thrill of flying changed to horror as he remembered his father's words. Icarus tried to work the pulleys to tilt his wings back down toward the sea, but they didn't respond. He saw more feathers falling from his wings, and he began to fall.

Icarus flapped the wings to try to slow his fall but the harder he flapped, the more feathers detached from the frame of his wings and the faster he fell toward the sea.

With tears streaming down his face, Daedalus shouted,

"Icarus! Icarus! I love you! Rise! Rise!" The inventor in him knew that there was no way Icarus could reverse the course he had set, but the father in him prayed for a miracle. It was too late. There were not enough feathers left to keep his son aloft.

As Daedalus watched in horror, Icarus crashed hard into the rough water, still frantically flapping the pulleys with his arms as he disappeared under the sea. Daedalus landed as quickly as he could on the beach near where Icarus had fallen, but the only sign of his son were a few feathers washing up on the beach.

Daedalus crumpled to the sand, his face in his hands. He knew his beloved son was dead. After many months, when Daedalus began to recover a little from his grief, he named the island Icaria, in memory of his son. On the beach where he landed, he built a temple to the sun god Apollo. Inside it hung the wings he had created, vowing never to fly again.

*
* *

Although history and myth don't tell us definitively if Daedalus ever flew again, it is certain that for the rest of his life he carried the pain of the death of his child.

The intimate connection between a parent and child always carries the possibility of being one of the most intense relationships in both of their lives. Though some parents and children disconnect from each other, that doesn't change the inherent potential of their relationship.

Most parents would risk or give their lives to save the lives of their children. There is something at the deepest level of human existence that impels a parent to protect their child, regardless of the danger to the parent.

Conversely, the death of a child is almost universally recognized as one of the most difficult and traumatic pains anyone could experience. Some pain never goes away. The best one can do is soften it and hope for healing with the passage of time. Daedalus would never be the same. The death of Icarus changed his life forever.

Why didn't Icarus heed Daedalus' admonishment to not fly too close to the sun or water? Icarus was foolish. He was impulsive. He was enthralled. To be enthralled can mean to be enslaved. It isn't simply fascination. When we are enthralled with distractions, lusts, stimuli or fascinations, we risk losing the ability to choose wisely.

Icarus was so enthralled he didn't even make a choice. He simply reacted. Wisdom had no opportunity to assert itself in his consciousness.

As he flew, he went from enthrallment to terror with no provision to ask the question *What is wise to do here?*

So often, that is the question that needs to be asked. *What is wise to do here? What actions, thoughts and deeds serve my destiny? Are there risks here that I haven't considered? Is this the right choice for me?*

When we do what is right for us, it is right for us. We must regularly ask the question of what is right and wrong for us and then align our actions with that truth.

To give wisdom an opportunity to influence us requires developing a habit of taking the time and creating the mental, emotional and spiritual space to ask and answer those questions.

Wisdom is never impulsive. It isn't hasty, though it can come swiftly. Wisdom includes the practice of going slow to go fast. The expression "Haste makes waste," represents foolishness. "A stitch in time saves nine," represents wisdom.

To be wise is to cultivate the practice of developing the discipline necessary to give wisdom an opportunity to influence our actions.

In every person, there is an extraordinary opportunity for wisdom to flourish. This opportunity is the birthright of all humans. It is available to everyone, though many haven't learned to use it.

Between every stimulus that enters our consciousness and our response to that impulse is the opportunity to exercise wisdom. For example, if you are a child and there is a piece of candy on the table that your parent said you must not eat until after dinner, you have the opportunity to behave wisely before your desire for sugar causes you to compulsively put the candy in your mouth because you want it right now!

Wisdom includes the capacity to recognize that even though we want to eat the candy now, if we do that there will be consequences. The practice of considering consequences before acting is wisdom. Wisdom almost always includes subordinating our impulses, or what we want right now, to whatever is genuinely good for us. Opportunity to practice wisdom always exists between stimulus and our response.

Human beings have natural impulses for food, sex, freedom, adventure, romance, acceptance and simply to "feel good." Learning to be wise about how we allow those impulses to determine our actions is wisdom. We need to eat, experience intimacy, feel loved, explore the world and do bold things. But we risk destroying ourselves when we act foolishly.

Too often, we respond to impulses without considering the consequences. We are free to choose our actions, but we aren't free to choose the consequences of what we do.

Practicing wisdom demands developing the habit of considering what we will do when we feel an impulse to do something and thinking about the possible consequences before we act.

This one habit can make so much difference in a person's life. It is a gateway to maturity and the doorway to inviting wisdom into our lives. All of us will fall short of the mark. There will be times that every person neglects to consider wisdom and acts impulsively, but the more we practice, the more we will choose wisely.

The expression to "fall short of the mark," comes from archery. To fall short of the mark means to miss hitting the bull's-eye, or the center of the target. It doesn't mean total failure. It only means that this time, with this single arrow, we didn't hit the center of the target. Sometimes we come very close to the center of the target, even if we miss the bull's-eye. That is progress!

Wisdom includes recognizing it is more important to be inspired by how close we came to hitting the bull's-eye, than feeling like a failure because we didn't perfectly hit the bull's-eye this time. Every time we shoot an arrow and hit or come close to the bull's-eye, we are making progress, and progress, not perfection, is an essential part of the human condition and every hero's journey.

To walk with dragons includes learning that when we don't hit the mark, we don't quit and we don't see ourselves as failures. Instead, we learn from our experience, and we get up and try again (though it's wise to take a break, have a nap, cry for our losses and get up again when we are rested).

To be true to our destiny and live our calling, we must

have wisdom in our lives. Two things are true of all men who walk with dragons: They follow a path that is true to their heart, and they are committed to trying to choose wisely.

CHAPTER NINE

LIVING YOUR CALLING

What is a calling? Some are easy to discern. For example, if we have children, or choose a spouse, we know we are called to be a parent or partner. It is impossible to be successful in other areas of life if we ignore the call to be a parent to our children, or betray a person we have committed ourselves to. No success in the outside world compensates for failure inside our home.

Some of us feel, often from a young age, a call to art, sports, medicine or designing and building things. If we are fortunate, we remember this as we grow older and learn to integrate the callings we remember from childhood into our adult lives.

When we successfully live the callings that we know are ours, we gain an ability to go deeper. This means we start to become aware of other callings that are meaningful but were obfuscated. This can happen at any time of life. Joan of Arc was a teenager when she was called to support France. Nelson Mandela was seventy-six-years old when he answered the call to become the president of South Africa, after having spent twenty-seven years in prison because of his commitment to supporting racial justice and equality.

While some callings are famous, most are not, but that doesn't make them any less important. Fame should rarely be used as a guide to whether something is important. While it is very human to esteem famous people and think we "aren't like them," the truth is that fame is almost never an indicator of whether a calling is right for us.

Callings are an "inside job." What the world will think of it isn't relevant or useful in discerning if a particular calling is ours to do. What will truly guide us is our intuition, wisdom, discernment and a growing ability to know that when something is right for us, it is right for us.

When I adopted my ten-year-old son from foster care, all the experts and many of my friends and family rightfully pointed out that I knew nothing about raising a troubled and neglected ten-year-old boy. From a logical perspective, adopting him made no sense. Moreover, my lack of experience and ability could have caused him more harm than good. I considered that. People I loved and trusted told me that if I adopted him that it would be the "worst decision you ever made." I did my best to consider what the people I trust and love told me.

But after considering what they said, I rejected their advice. Fortunately for my son and me, I had acquired enough emotional and spiritual maturity that while I considered the advice of others, I didn't feel compelled to follow it. I listen to the people I love and trust. But at the same time I was being told by others not to adopt him, my heart sang daily, "This is your destiny. This is yours to do."

I knew at the deepest level of my soul that even though nothing could force me to adopt him, that if I didn't create a family with him, I had missed the mark. I had failed to answer my call. I knew this was mine to do and that if I failed at this no other success I would ever achieve would compensate for failing to answer this call. I had the wisdom, intuition, discernment and integrity to choose to become his dad despite trusted influences in my life telling me this was a mistake.

As much as I loved and trusted the people I am closest to, I trusted my inner guidance more than I trusted their advice. It was the right decision. More than a decade later, everyone who suggested I shouldn't have adopted him agrees now it was the exact right decision.

I could not have made that decision if I hadn't learned to trust my intuition, practice integrity, develop my wisdom, and learned to discern what matters most. I love the idea of "practicing" integrity, as the word practice means we are still learning to do it.

When we learn to play the piano, we practice it. We learn to play scales. Often our early efforts sound discordant to others, but it is in our mistakes that we learn to improve and play better. Eventually, if we keep at it, one day we can surprise and inspire friends and family by playing a beautiful piece of music that touches their heart.

But it takes a long time to learn to play something well. Practicing is the practice of making mistakes, learning from them, and then trying again, over and over, until usually after a long time we get better and better. We are never perfect, but we are much improved. Integrity is a practice. Until our last day on earth, we will still be trying to do it better.

What I learned from adopting my son is that some decisions must be made from the heart, not the head. They are best made from my inner world than from the messages and communication from the outer world. But to learn to make decisions from my "inner world," I had to learn to walk with dragons and become comfortable in that world too.

The longer I live, the more I believe that the most significant decisions I make are best made from the heart, not the head. My head is wonderful for deciding which mortgage and interest rate to accept if I am buying a home, but in matters of the soul and calling, my heart has proved a more reliable guide.

Too often, we choose to accept or reject callings based on what we think others will think of us, or from a desire to "fit in," be popular or to avoid the hard work of change and growth that comes from answering a true calling.

When we choose a calling that is right for us, dragons will walk with us. They love authentic paths! They are as impressed and inspired as we are when any of us fulfill our destiny. Conversely, they mourn, as we do, when the promise inherent in every being as we came to earth "trailing clouds of glory" is squandered in the darkness of apathy, overwhelmingness and grief.

In the story of *The Fir Tree*, we can see how easy it is to squander a life, and how painful it is to realize this after it's too late to choose differently.

THE FIR TREE

Out in the woods stood a pretty little fir tree. It grew in a good place, where it had plenty of sun and fresh air. Around it stood many tall comrades, both fir trees and pines.

The little fir tree was in a hurry to grow up. It didn't care a thing for the warm sunshine, or the fresh air, and it took no interest in the children who ran about chattering when they came to pick wild berries. Often, when the children had picked their pails full, they would sit down to rest near the little fir. "Oh, isn't it a nice little tree?" they said. "It's the baby of the woods." The little tree didn't like their remarks at all. A baby was not what the little tree aspired to be.

After a year of four seasons, it shot up a joint of new growth. The following year another joint grew, a bit longer.

"I wish I were a grown-up tree, like the big trees around me," the little tree sighed. "If I were grown-up, I could stretch out my branches and see from my top what the world is like. The birds would make me their nesting place, and when the wind blew I could sway back and forth with all the other great trees."

The little tree took no pleasure in the sunshine nor in the birds. The radiant clouds that sailed overhead at sunrise and sunset meant nothing to it.

In winter, when the snow lay sparkling on the ground, a rabbit would often come hopping along and jump right over the little tree. Oh, how irritating that was! That happened for two winters, but when the third winter came the tree was so tall that the rabbit had to turn aside and hop around it.

Oh, I want to grow! I need to get older and taller, the little tree thought. *To grow old and be tall and powerful is the most wonderful thing in this world. I hate who I am and being small.*

In the autumn, woodcutters came and cut down a few of the largest trees. This happened every year. The young fir was no longer a baby tree, and it trembled to see how those stately great trees crashed to the ground, how their limbs were lopped off, and how lean they looked as their naked trunks were loaded into carts. It hardly recognized the trees it had known when they left the woods.

Where were they going? What would become of them? The young tree wondered.

In the springtime, when swallows and herons came back, the tree asked them, "Do you know where the other trees went? Have you met them?"

The swallows knew nothing about it, but the heron

looked thoughtful and nodded his head. "Yes, I think I met them," he said. "On my way from across the water, I saw many new ships, and some had tall, stately masts. They may well have been the trees you mean."

"Oh, I wish I were old enough to travel on the sea! Please tell me what it really is and how it looks."

"That would take too long to tell," said the heron, and off he went.

"Rejoice in your youth," said the sunbeams. "Take pride in your growing strength and in the stir of life within you." But the young tree didn't listen to them at all.

The wind kissed the tree, and the dew wept over it, but the tree was young and without understanding of the riches of the forest and how time was quickly passing.

When Christmas came near, many young trees were cut down. Some were not even as old or as tall as the young fir tree, who was in such a hurry to grow up and go traveling. These young trees, which were always the handsomest ones, had their branches left on them when they were loaded on carts and then taken out of the woods.

"Where can they be going?" the fir tree wondered aloud. "They are no taller than I am. One was really much smaller than I am. And why are they allowed to keep all their branches? Where can they be going?"

"We know! We know!" the sparrows chirped. "We have been to town and peeped in the windows. We know where they are going. The greatest splendor and glory you can imagine awaits them. We've seen them planted right in the middle of a warm room, and decked out with the most splendid things—gold apples, gingerbread, toys and many hundreds of lights."

"And then?" asked the fir tree, trembling in every twig. "And then? What happens then?"

"We saw nothing more. And never have we seen anything that could match it."

I wonder if I was created for such a glorious future?" The fir tree wondered. *Why, that is better than to cross the sea. I'm tormented with longing. I want to be planted in the middle of a warm room and get decorated and surrounded by wonderful things. Oh, if Christmas would only come! I'm just as tall and grown-up as the trees they chose last year. How I wish I were already in the cart, on my way to the warm room where there's so much splendor and glory. I know that after I am planted in the warm room and decorated, something even better, something still more important is bound to happen, or why should they make me so fine? Yes, there must be something still grander! But what? I don't know what's the matter with me. It's not fair that the other trees get to enjoy the beautiful warm room and I am stuck in this boring forest.*

"Enjoy us while you may," the air and sunlight told him. "Rejoice in the days of your youth, out here in the open. Where you are is where you are meant to be, and what is around you is better than you think."

But the tree did not rejoice at all. It just grew. It grew and stayed dark green both winter and summer. People who passed it said, "There's a beautiful tree!" The young tree was happy to hear their praise.

When Christmastime came again, they cut it down first. The ax struck deep into its trunk. The tree sighed as it fell to the ground. It felt faint with pain. Instead of the happiness it had expected, the tree was sorry to leave the home where it had grown up. It knew that never again would it see its dear old comrades, the little bushes and the flowers about it, and perhaps not even the birds. The departure was anything but pleasant.

The tree did not get over it until all the trees were unloaded in the yard, and it heard a man say, "That's a splendid one. That's the tree for us." A short time later, the fir tree came into a big splendid drawing room. Magnificent artwork hung all around the walls. On either side of the fireplace stood great Chinese vases, with lions on the lids of them. There were easy chairs, luxurious sofas and long tables strewn with picture books, and with toys that were worth a lot of money, or so the children said.

The fir tree was planted in a large tub filled with sand, but no one could see that it was a tub, because it was wrapped in a rich green cloth and set on a thick carpet. How the tree quivered! What would come next? Many people helped attach the fine decorations. From its branches they hung little nets cut out of colored paper, and each net was filled with candies. Gilded apples and walnuts hung in clusters as if they grew there, and a hundred little white, blue, green and red lights were fastened to its twigs. Among its green branches swayed dolls that it took to be real living people, for the tree had never seen dolls before. Up at its very top was set a large gold star. It was splendid beyond all words and everything the tree had ever imagined.

I have finally arrived, the young tree thought. *I am beautiful and adored, and I can't imagine what wonderful things will happen to me after this. It is so good to leave the dark, wet forest and live in splendor!*

"Tonight," everyone said, "ah, tonight how the tree will shine!"

Oh, thought the tree, *if tonight would only come! I look so much more radiant when the lights are lit! And after that, what happens then? Will the trees come trooping out of the woods to see me? Will the sparrows flock to the windows? Shall I take root here, and stand in fine ornaments all winter and summer long?*

That was how much the tree knew about its future. All its longing had gone to its bark and set it to arching, which is as bad for a tree as a headache is for a person.

That evening the lights were lit. What sparkling splendor! What a blaze of light! Its own brilliance dazzled it.

Suddenly, the folding doors were thrown back, and a whole flock of children burst in as if they would overturn the tree completely. Their elders marched in after them, more sedately. For a moment, but only for a moment, the young ones were stricken speechless. Then they shouted till the rafters rang. They danced about the tree and plucked off one present after another.

What are they up to? the tree wondered. *What will happen next?*

Soon all the presents were removed from the tree and the children danced about with their splendid playthings. No one looked at the tree now.

"Tell us a story! Tell us a story!" the children clamored, as they towed a fat little man to the tree. He sat down beneath it and said, "Here we are in the woods, and it will do the tree a lot of good to listen to our story. Mind you, I'll tell only one. Which will you have, the story of Sleeping Beauty, or the one about Humpty-Dumpty who tumbled downstairs, yet ascended the throne and married the princess?"

"Sleeping Beauty," cried some. "Humpty-Dumpty," cried the others. And there was a great amount of noise. Only the fir tree held its peace, though it thought to itself, *Am I to be left out of this? Isn't there anything I can do?* For earlier all the fun of the evening had centered upon it, and it had played its part well, but now it felt forgotten.

The fat little man told them all about Humpty-Dumpty, who tumbled downstairs, yet ascended the throne and married the princess. And the children clapped and shouted, "Tell us another one! Tell us another one!" For they wanted to hear about Sleeping Beauty too, but after Humpty-Dumpty the story telling stopped. The fir tree stood very still as it pondered how the birds in the woods had never told it a story to equal this.

Humpty-Dumpty tumbled downstairs, yet he married the

princess. Imagine! That must be how things happen in the world. You never can tell. Maybe I'll tumble downstairs and marry a princess too, thought the fir tree, which believed every word of the story because such a nice man had told it.

The tree looked forward to the following day, when they would put presents under it again, *Tomorrow I shall hear about Humpty-Dumpty again, and perhaps Sleeping Beauty too.* All night long the tree stood silent as it dreamed its dreams, and the next morning people started cleaning the room.

Now my splendor will be renewed, the fir tree thought. But they dragged the tree downstairs to the basement, and there they left it in a dark corner where no daylight ever came. *What's the meaning of this?* the tree wondered. *What am I going to do here? What stories shall I hear?* It leaned against the wall, lost in dreams. It had plenty of time for dreaming, as the days and the nights went by. Nobody came to the basement. And when at last someone did come, it was only to put many big boxes away in the corner. The tree was quite hidden. One might think it had been entirely forgotten.

It's still winter outside, the tree thought. *The earth is too hard and covered with snow for them to plant me now. I must have been put here for shelter until springtime comes. How thoughtful of them! How good people are! Only, I wish it weren't so dark here, and so very, very lonely. There's not even a little rabbit. It was so friendly out in the woods when the snow was on the ground and the rabbit came hopping along. Yes, he was friendly even when he jumped right over me, though I did not think so then. Here it's all so terribly lonely.*

"Squeak, squeak!" said a little mouse just then. He crept across the floor, and another one followed him. They sniffed the fir tree, and rustled in and out among its branches.

"It is fearfully cold," one of them said. "Except for that, it would be very nice here, wouldn't it, you old fir tree?"

"I'm not at all old," said the fir tree. "Many trees are much older than I am."

"Where did you come from?" the mice asked him. "And what do you know?" They were most inquisitive creatures.

"Tell us about the most beautiful place in the world. Have you been there? Were you ever in the kitchen, where there are cheeses and bread? It's the place where you can dart in thin and squeeze out fat."

"I know nothing of that place," said the tree. "But I know the woods where the sun shines and the little birds sing." Then it told them about its youth. The little mice had never heard the like of it. They listened very intently and said, "My! How much you have seen! And how happy it must have made you."

"I?" the fir tree thought about it. "Yes, those days were rather amusing." And he went on to tell them about Christmas Eve, when it was decorated with presents, ornaments, candies and lights.

"Oh," said the little mice, "how lucky you have been, you old fir tree!"

"I am not at all old," it insisted. "I came out of the woods just this winter, and I'm really in the prime of life, though at the moment my growth is suspended."

"How nicely you tell things," said the mice. The next night they came with four other mice to hear what the tree had to say. The more it talked, the more clearly it recalled things, and it thought, *Those were happy times. But they may still come back—they may come back again. Humpty-Dumpty fell downstairs, and yet he married the princess. Maybe the same thing will happen to me.* The fir tree thought about a charming little birch tree that grew out in the woods. To the fir tree, she was a real and lovely princess.

"Who is Humpty-Dumpty?" the mice asked it. So the fir tree told them the whole story, for it could remember it word by word. The little mice were ready to jump to the top of the tree for joy. The next night, many more mice came to see the fir tree. On Sunday, two rats paid it a call, but they said that the story was not very amusing. This made the little mice so sad that they began to find it not so very interesting either.

"Is that the only story you know?" the rats asked.

"Only that one," the tree answered. "I heard it on the happiest evening of my life, but I did not know then how happy I was."

"It's a very silly story. Don't you know one that tells about bacon and cheese? Can't you tell us a good kitchen story with lots of crunchings and munchings?"

"No," said the tree.

"Goodbye then, and we won't be back," the rats said, and they went away.

At last the little mice took to staying away too. The tree thought, *Oh, wasn't it pleasant when those friendly little mice sat around and listened to all that I had to say. Now that too is past and gone. But I will take good care to enjoy myself, once they let me out of here.*

When would that be? Finally, one morning people came down to clean out the basement. The boxes were moved, the tree was pulled out and thrown hard on the floor. But soon it was dragged near the stairway, where there was daylight again.

Now my life will start all over, the tree thought. It felt the fresh air and the first sunbeam strike it as it came out into the yard. This all happened so quickly and there was so much going around it, that the tree forgot to give even a glance at itself. The lovely yard adjoined a garden, where flowers were blooming. Great masses of fragrant roses hung over a picket fence. The linden trees were in blossom, and between them the swallows skimmed past.

Now I shall live again, it rejoiced, and tried to stretch out its branches. Alas, they were withered, and brown, and brittle. It was tossed into a corner, among weeds and nettles. But the gold star that was still tied to its top sparkled bravely in the sunlight.

Several of the merry children, who had danced around the tree and taken such pleasure in it at Christmas, were playing outside. One of the youngest seized upon it and tore off the star.

"Look what is still hanging on that ugly old dead Christmas tree," the child said, and stamped upon the branches until they cracked beneath his shoes.

The tree saw the beautiful flowers blooming freshly in the garden. It saw itself, and wished that they had left it in the darkest corner of the cellar. It thought of its own young days in the deep woods, and of the merry Christmas Eve, and of the little mice who had been so pleased when it told them the story of Humpty-Dumpty.

My days are over and past, mourned the poor tree. *Why didn't I enjoy them while I could? Now they are gone. I was such a fool.*

A man came and chopped the tree into little pieces. These heaped together quite high. The wood blazed beautifully in the fireplace of the great room where months before the tree had been decorated and lived the most memorable night of its life. The fir tree moaned so deeply that each groan sounded like a muffled shot.

The children who were playing nearby ran to the fireplace, stared into the fire and cried "BOOM! BOOM!" But as each groan burst from it, the tree thought of a bright summer day in the woods, or a starlit winter night. It thought of Christmas Eve and thought of Humpty-Dumpty, which was the only story it ever heard and knew how to tell. And soon the tree was burned completely away.

The children played on in the courtyard. The youngest child wore on his breast the gold star that had topped the tree on its happiest night of all. But that was no more, and the tree was no more, and there's no more to my story. No more, nothing more. All stories come to an end.

Joni Mitchell famously sang, "You don't know what you've got till it's gone." This revelation has haunted so many of us.

In childhood and adolescence most of us want to be big! Grown-up! Adult! In the earlier stages of life, we generally believe that when we are older we will have more material things, more autonomy, and we will learn the mysteries the adults know that we don't.

Often the realization comes in young adulthood that life when we were younger actually wasn't so bad. We generally didn't have many bills to pay, the pressures in our daily life came from parents and schools, not employers, spouses and our children.

For many of us, as we grow older life gets harder and more complex. Henry Thoreau wrote that most men, "lead lives of quiet desperation." What did he mean? He meant that most men suffer from the weight of societal, personal and family expectations and that they often secretly believe that they can't measure up. So they spend their lives trying not to get "found out" as failures as they try to live up to the expectations they believe they need to live up to, to be "real" men.

The escape from the emotional and spiritual pain of trying to live up to these artificial expectations is often found in mindless television, alcohol and other intoxicants, sex without intimacy and anything else that will allow the mind to be free of anxiety and worry if only for a short time. Over time, most of us discover that these short-term panaceas are merely pacifiers for the mind. They don't change anything. They don't bring meaning or fulfillment to our lives. They often harm us and they don't offer hope.

The tree was almost never happy. As a young tree, every desire and thought was to grow older, take root somewhere else and have a better existence. The everyday beauty of its natural environment was ignored, and replaced by a fantasy of living in a house, becoming decorated and finding some grand existence after that.

When the tree's ambition was fulfilled and it had a day of glory, it discovered the awful truth that there was nothing that followed the elaborate decorations. The tree's ultimate fate was to be discarded, abandoned and destroyed.

The tree's fate is a powerful example of what happens when we don't use wisdom to discover our calling. While some callings are more profound or demanding than others, all of us miss some opportunities. We are human.

We make mistakes. Fortunately, life constantly offers opportunities. If you have ever wondered if it is too late to fulfill your life's calling; if you are alive it isn't. If we are alive on this earth, there is always some way we can serve.

Why should we do that? What is the point of serving others? Whether one is an atheist or a devout follower of a great religion or ideology, the giving of one's resources and abilities for the common good of all brings meaning to our lives.

A gift of learning to walk with a dragon is to live a life of meaning. While happiness and joy feel good, a life devoted solely to their pursuit will inevitably fail. Even the most cursory consideration of life reveals that existence on this planet will always come with some amount of grief, loss, disappointment and betrayal. Fortunately, life also brings us joy, happiness, grace and love.

The surest path to walk with a dragon is to commit to living a life that has meaning. To do that requires that when destiny knocks on our door, we answer the door and accept the call. The more we do this, the more calls we receive, and the more opportunities we will be given to serve this beautiful, flawed, needy world that we all share.

CHAPTER TEN

SACRED

Men who walk with dragons see the sacred in the ordinary.

Much of the day-to-day life that whirls around us revolves around going to work, getting money, taking care of those we are responsible for, and repeating that every day.

It is easy to lose sight of the sacred as we are mired in the ordinary activities of daily life. Our connection to the sacred is a bridge to incredible resources, including love, kindness and grace. It isn't possible to live our destiny without a healthy reverence for the sacred.

Reverence stems from the word *revere*. To revere something is to value or esteem it. We often revere our parents, ancestors or others who love, support and encourage us. Many revere the divine, including what some call God, Goddess, Higher Power or Creator. We must learn to serve something other than ourselves, or life is ultimately meaningless.

A fundamental truth of human existence, and a reason dragons will walk with us, is that we are destined to serve that which is greater. Usually that comes in the form of serving those around us. Ironically, it is through serving others that we ourselves mature.

There is a reason that heroes always stop to serve others. Much of the success of any quest isn't found solely from reaching a destination. It is in how one travels and comports oneself when living one's calling.

Traveling a path true to our heart is one way to stay aligned with the sacred. The sacred tends to reveal itself through the heart, through deep feelings, as the truth of the sacred usually transcends logic, rational thought and the approbation of the world. The sacred stamps our soul so intensely, that we know when we are in its presence, that it is right for us. To deny it is a betrayal of all that is right, true, holy and wise. To deny the sacred after it is revealed to us is a dark, painful path. Although recovery is possible, it is hard.

The relationship of a grandparent and grandchild always carries the potential to be sacred. They usually both love and revere each other.

Their relationship is inherently short-lived, as grandchildren and grandparents have a generation between them, so their time together on earth is usually shorter than either of them desire.

The bonds that connect the closest of people are sacred. Because we are human and we have bad days, hurt feelings, anxieties, depressions, fears and countless other challenges, too often we profane the sacred. We desecrate the people who love us as we falter in our efforts to live up to our best selves.

If we are fortunate, our loved ones are wise, understanding and forgiving. But sometimes, we banish the sacred in outbursts of anger, violence, ill-considered words and other inflicted wounds. Sometimes those who experience our wrath can't or won't forgive or understand us.

It is important to keep the sacred, sacred. To walk with dragons, we must respect, revere and love that which is holy. As our understanding of what is holy expands, it becomes possible to see the world and all her inhabitants as sacred.

When we ignore the sacred and avert our eyes from suffering children, the aged, the sick, prisoners, and those dwelling in lowly places, we diminish and sometimes lose our ability to connect to the sacred, and what truly matters most.

We must be kind to each other. We must feed the hungry, clothe the naked, care for the sick, comfort the troubled and remember that to serve others is always part of our calling. To walk with dragons requires that we act as heroes, that we become each other's angels. No quest is successful if we abandon our obligation to do what is in our reach and serve those in need who surround us.

In the story of *The Little Match Girl*, we can see what happens when no mortal serves or helps a young girl in great need.

THE LITTLE MATCH GIRL

The night was terribly cold. It snowed and was quite dark, and this evening was the last night of the year. In this cold and darkness was a poor little girl, bareheaded and with naked feet. When she left home she had slippers on. The slippers belonged to her mother and were much too large for her young feet. She lost them as she crossed the street and had to run because two carriages rolled by and nearly hit her.

One slipper disappeared and the other was stolen by a boy. The little girl walked in the cold, dark night through the snow with her tiny, naked feet. Her feet were red and blue from cold.

Her family was quite poor. Her mother told her she must sell matches as they needed the money to eat. "People will feel sorry for you," she told her daughter. "Strangers will give money to a little girl that they won't give to me." She was a good girl who minded her mother, so she carried matches in an old apron, and she held a bundle of them in her hand and offered them to strangers. Nobody had bought anything from her this day. She hadn't received a farthing or a cent.

She crept along, trembling with cold and hunger, the very picture of sorrow. She was so cold that she started to forget how devastating her circumstances were. The frigid temperature in the night started robbing her of common sense as her feet and fingers grew numb.

Flakes of snow covered her long dark hair, which fell in beautiful curls around her neck, but she wasn't mindful of her beauty. She only knew she was hungry and cold.

From windows along the street, she saw candles gleaming, and smells of roast goose, potatoes and pie, for it was New Year's Eve. She looked longingly at the warm rooms from which the wonderful smells came. She wasn't envious or jealous. She only wondered why it seemed everyone else could have the warmth and food she could not.

In a corner formed by two houses, she seated herself down and cowered as she curled her body in the snow. She shivered for a moment. She drew her little feet close up to her, but she grew colder and colder.

She was afraid to go home and disappoint her mother. She had not sold any matches and could not bring home any money. If her father were home, she would certainly get blows, especially if he had managed to find spirits to drink. Her home was cold too, though not as cold as this, for above her she had only the roof, through which the wind whistled and the rain fell, even though the largest cracks were stopped up with straw and rags.

Her little hands were numb with cold. A sudden and dangerous thought occurred to her. Oh! A match might afford her a world of comfort, if she only dared take a single one out of the bundle, draw it against the wall, and warm her fingers by the flame. Feeling daring and desperate, she drew one out. How it sizzled and blazed and burnt! It was a warm, bright flame, like a candle, as she held her hands over it. It was a wonderful light. It seemed almost divine.

As the flame flickered, she imagined she were sitting before a large iron stove, with burnished brass feet and a brass ornament at top. The fire burned with unfettered generosity and warmed her and her family delightfully. The little girl stretched out her feet to warm them too, but the small flame went out and the stove vanished. She sat in the cold snow with only the remains of the burned-out match in her hand.

I must do it again she thought. She rubbed another match against the wall. It burned brightly, and where the light fell on the wall, the wall became transparent like a veil, so that she could see into the room. On the table was spread a snow-white tablecloth. Upon it were splendid goblets and plates, and a roast goose was steaming with its stuffing of apple and dried plums. And what was magical to behold was the goose knew she was tired, and hungry and couldn't move herself. She saw the goose hop down from the dish, reeled about on the floor with knife and fork in its breast, and it came up to her to nourish and warm her.

But the match went out and nothing but the thick, cold, damp wall and snow beneath her remained. She lit another match. Now she was sitting under the most magnificent Christmas tree. It was still larger, and more decorated than the one that she had seen through the glass door in the rich merchant's house.

Hundreds of lights were burning on the green branches, and colorful pictures, such as she had seen in the shop windows, looked down upon her. The little girl stretched out her hands toward them, but the match went out. As the light and warmth of the match receded, the lights of the Christmas tree rose higher and higher. She saw them now as stars in heaven. One fell down and formed a long trail of fire.

"Someone is just dead!" said the little girl, for her old grandmother, the only person who had loved her, and who was now no more, had told her that when a star falls a soul ascends to God.

She drew another match against the wall. It was again light, and in the soft glow stood her old grandmother. The person she loved above all people, and the woman who had always loved and comforted her in return. She was so bright and radiant, so mild, and her eyes and countenance were a perfect expression of light and love.

"Grandmother!" cried the little one. "Oh, Grandmother. You look so good! You are healed! I knew you wouldn't die and you would come back for me! Please, take me with you! Please don't go away when the match burns out. Please don't vanish like the warm stove, the roast goose, and the magnificent Christmas tree! I need you, Grandmother. I need you!" She started crying. Her heart couldn't stand to be separated from her grandmother ever again.

In a burst of defiance and bringing all of her will to bear to keep her grandmother with her forever, she rubbed the whole bundle of matches quickly against the wall.

The matches gave such a brilliant light that it seemed brighter than at noonday. Never had her beloved grandmother been so beautiful or tall. Her grandmother looked at her with eyes full of love, and lifted her into a warm and tight embrace, and both flew in brightness and in joy so high, so very high, that there was neither cold, nor hunger, nor anxiety. They were with God.

But in the corner, at the cold hour of dawn, sat a poor girl, with rosy cheeks and a smiling mouth, leaning against the wall, frozen to death on the last evening of the old year. Stiff and stark sat the child there with her matches, of which the large bundle had been burned. "She wanted to warm herself," people said. No one had the slightest suspicion of what beautiful things she had seen. No one even dreamed of the splendor into which, with her grandmother, she had entered on the joys of a new year.

In our deepest, hardest times, there is always something there to support us, guide us, nurture us and love us. But we must learn to recognize it.

For many humans, the love from a grandparent is one of their greatest sources of security. Not all grandparents are kind, not everyone had living grandparents they could spend time with. But many do. In the same way that not all parents are the biological progenitors of their children, not all grandparents fulfill the role of family elder in a traditional way.

To walk with dragons means that one day we arrive in a place of elderhood. Communities and loved ones need "wise adults." Inside themselves, elders still carry many of the same hopes, fears, dreams and anxieties they had as children, teenagers and young adults. But that isn't how the world sees them, nor is it the role they are called to live now.

The day will come, if we are fortunate enough to live many decades, and if we answer our callings and strive to fulfill our quests, that we will become elders.

Elderhood and grandparenting are spiritually connected to the same root. We don't need to have a grandchild to be an elder, nor is it wise to avoid our duties as an elder with our grandchildren.

One way to consider what it means to walk with dragons is to live a full life, answer our callings, commit ourselves to valuing meaning over happiness, work our way through the inevitable pain, grief and sorrow that is part of our human condition, and then arrive at elderhood prepared to serve others and communicate what we have learned.

In the Middle Ages, there were great cathedrals whose creation took many decades or even centuries. The men who designed and planned the cathedrals knew they would never see them completed, but they did their part, trusting that the great work they were committed to would be a legacy for generations to come.

Men who walk with dragons understand that the farmers don't always see the harvests they planted, or the gardeners the magnificent sight of the trees they toiled to grow. Parents and grandparents don't get to see much of the fruit of the legacy they plant in their children, or those they mentor and love. Yet, they still do it. It is sacred work.

To walk with dragons means looking through a lens that is different than the day-to-day view used to navigate the ordinary world. It requires using a lens that considers the spiritual and the greater good of all humanity. It means being thoughtful of the generations of children and grandchildren, great-grandchildren and great-great-grandchildren who follow us, and to carry on the good legacies of our forebearers.

Elders and grandparents are way-showers. Guides. They help others navigate life with wisdom and encourage their growth. They don't judge others so much as work with them exactly where they are. They tend to see challenging behaviors less as problems to be solved than as facts that will lead to finding solutions.

For example, if a river constantly overflows a dam, is that a problem to get angry about or to blame others for causing? Is it wise to curse the engineer or builder who didn't provide a sufficient structure to stem the flow of the river, or can we simply see the challenge as a fact? Once we accept that water flows over the structure, it seems obvious that seeking solutions is wise.

In many situations, it is far more important to find solutions than to seek blame and complain about the mistakes of the past. Much of the value in mistakes comes from learning from them and not repeating them, not rehashing and staying stuck in them.

Men who walk with dragons aren't victims. They understand that the life they are living and their reaction to their circumstances is a result of their choices and attitudes. While they understand that often "life isn't fair," and tragedy befalls them and their loved ones, they don't blame the universe or wallow in self-pity. Instead, they do what is within their reach to improve the circumstances around them. Men who walk with dragons are healers.

The grandmother in this story healed her granddaughter from the cold life she was in. It wasn't just the snow on the ground. It was the absence of love in her life. Perhaps the grandmother couldn't stop the little match girl from dying in the cold. There are some natural laws that even challenge the angels. But she could make it better. She could "soften the blow," by making sure when it was time for her granddaughter's soul to separate from her body and go to whatever great mystery follows death, that she could guide, accompany, encourage and love her.

One of the messages of *The Little Match Girl* is that love transcends death. And while the love of a parent for a child is great, the love of an elder or grandparent can be as powerful a force of love as anything known to us. There is something unique about the love from an elder that transcends the mind and connects straight to the heart and soul.

The sense of security, comfort, safety and peace that comes from this love is the holy grail of relationships. To walk with dragons is to prepare oneself to not only serve our callings and destiny, but to prepare for the day that we serve others in ways that are beyond what we can imagine today.

All of us are wounded. Whether we came to life with wounds or quickly acquired them isn't as important as understanding that we all have been hurt. Painful and traumatic things happen to each of us.

One of the most important lessons of walking with a dragon is to learn to transmute the wounds to healing. The ultimate alchemy isn't to turn lead into gold. It's to turn Thanatos [death] to Eros [life], hate to love, suffering to joy, abandonment to connection, and to let the seed of destiny within each of us grow and guide us into whatever wild, beautiful, divine being we were always destined to be.

Walking with dragons isn't for the faint of heart. There is much suffering on any quest, and even if we don't suffer pain personally, empathy and consciousness demand that we share the pain felt by others.

The path of destiny we walk with dragons is sacred. This means it is not only holy, blessed and inspired; it is unknowable.

It requires an act of faith to accept that we may never fully understand in this life why we do what we are called to do, or how our actions serve others. But that doesn't matter. We do the work not to seek recognition or praise, but because it is our sacred work to do, and we are the ones uniquely able to do it.

It can be hard to answer a call to serve without getting to experience the fruits that come from the labor, or the joy of interacting with others we are helping. But even though the path is often lonely, murky and mysterious, the grace of walking with a dragon includes the awareness that we are never walking alone.

Chapter Eleven

BECOMING A HERO

Most boys and men want to be heroes. They want to fight injustice, protect the vulnerable, rescue the endangered and make the world a better place.

But it's hard to be a hero. Heroes are targets for predators and villains. Being a hero is often lonely, and it requires doing difficult things.

The greatest challenge to being a hero isn't the dangers or the improbable odds of success. It's our belief we aren't good enough, that we lack what it takes to be heroic, and the fear that something in us is flawed or incapable of heroic behavior.

Whether we think we aren't strong enough, smart enough, lucky or brave enough, there is almost always a reason we think we aren't capable of being a hero.

Too often heroes are perceived as brave, flawless, perfect men who succeed in whatever they set out to do.

The truth about heroes is simple: The world is filled with them. It is heroic to be a twenty-two-year-old and walk to work because you had to spend your gas money on diapers. It's heroic to stop drinking alcohol and other drugs. It's heroic to have a good attitude while your body is battling cancer.

Opportunities for heroism abound. When we walk with dragons, our inner hero emerges. In the story of *The Brave Little Tailor*, a man is initially mistakenly perceived as a hero, but as his journey continues he starts to accomplish true heroic deeds.

THE BRAVE LITTLE TAILOR

Once upon a time, there was a man who worked as a tailor. He enjoyed his craft and had gotten so proficient with his hands that he often daydreamed about what he might do if he weren't repairing and creating clothes for others.

One afternoon, while eating a lunch of jam and bread, he noticed a swarm of flies circling his sandwich. "Hey! Get away from there!" he called.

Grabbing a piece of cloth, he swatted the flies with all his might. Laying on the table was a row of dead, black corpses. "One. Two. Three," he counted, "Four. Five. Six. Seven! I killed seven in a blow!" A surge of pride flowed through him.

"I need to tell everyone! Whoever heard of killing seven in a blow." He grabbed his favorite jacket and quickly embroidered "SEVEN IN A BLOW" in large letters on the back of it.

Feeling overwhelmed by his success, he put on his

jacket, grabbed an orange and a knapsack, and left his shop to tell the world of his achievement.

As he walked on the trail, he saw a small bird trapped in a thistle. He rescued it and placed it in his pocket to rest and heal.

Soon he saw a giant sitting on the side of the road. "Ho, Giant," the tailor called. "I'm out to tell the world of my great achievement. Would you like to join me?"

"Join you?" the giant scoffed. "You're lucky I don't eat you."

"You have sorely misjudged me," the tailor answered. He turned around so the giant could read the words on his jacket.

The giant read SEVEN IN A BLOW and thinking the tailor had killed seven men, he gained some respect for the little fellow. "Hmmph! Well, maybe you are a little stronger than you appear," said the giant. "But a scrawny little fellow like you isn't able to do this!" The giant picked up a stone and squeezed it so hard that water dripped from it.

"I do that for exercise," said the little tailor. He reached in his pocket, pulled out the orange and squeezed it until it dripped even more than the giant's stone.

The giant, whose vision was as poor as his temper, grabbed a rock and said, "I'd like to see you do this!" And he threw the stone so high that it almost went out of sight before returning to the ground.

"That was a good throw," the tailor admitted, "but it did come back. I'll throw one so high you will never see it again." He pulled the bird he rescued from his pocket and threw it in the air. The bird, feeling happy to be free, flew away. "What do you think of that?" he asked the giant.

"You throw pretty well," the giant admitted, "but let's see if you have real strength." He led the tailor to an oak tree that had been cut down. "If you are strong enough, help me carry this tree out of the woods."

"I'll gladly do that," the tailor said. "You take the trunk on your shoulder and I will carry the branches and twigs since they are the heaviest part."

The giant lifted the trunk onto his shoulder, but the tailor sat on a branch. Because the giant couldn't see well, he didn't realize he was dragging the tree with the little tailor sitting on it.

The giant grew tired and finally said, "Let's stop. I need a short rest."

"A rest! What is wrong with you? I could go for miles like this," the little tailor said.

"Fine!" The giant shouted. "If you're so strong and brave, then come to our cave and spend the night with us."

"Gladly," the little tailor said. "I was wondering where I would sleep tonight," and he followed the giant home.

When they reached the cave, other giants were sitting by a fire. Each had roasted meat in their hands and were gnawing on it. Soon, the giant showed him a bed and told him to lie down and go to sleep. The tailor found the bed too large, so instead of lying there he hid in the corner. At midnight, the giant believing the tailor was fast asleep, crept up to the bed and smashed it in two with a large iron bar. *He wasn't so strong* the giant thought, as he himself went to bed.

The next morning, the giants went into the woods, when suddenly the little tailor appeared.

"Thank you for your hospitality," he said. The giants were so frightened to see him alive, they scattered into the woods. The tailor helped himself to some of their treasures and proceeded down the road.

Near nightfall, he came upon the courtyard of a palace and, being tired, he lay down in the grass and slept. In the morning, some soldiers and servants saw him, but when they approached and read SEVEN IN A BLOW on his jacket, they let him rest, thinking he was a great hero.

The king was told that a hero was resting in the courtyard. He knew it was wise to make this hero welcome, for even though his land was mostly at peace, the threats of danger and war always existed and strong, powerful men were rare.

The king sent one of his generals to speak to the tailor and offer him a position in the king's army.

"Hello," said the general. "What brings a brave hero like you to our kingdom? Our king is hoping that you might be willing to join our army. There's always a place for brave men like you."

"That sounds excellent," the tailor answered. The general was relieved, as he was scared of the little man who had killed seven in a blow.

The tailor was given private quarters, as none of the other soldiers wanted to live with him. They were afraid of his strength and didn't want him to become angry with them.

Soon all the soldiers went to the general and said, "Who can stand up to him, this man who killed seven in a blow? Please tell the king we must be released from his service as we can't risk making him angry and having him kill us too!"

The general told the king. Realizing he had a problem, the king decided he must send the tailor away from the other men, but he couldn't risk upsetting the tailor and having him attack his kingdom.

He thought long and hard of how he might find a solution, and then he remembered that in a nearby forest, there lived two giants who caused great damage. They were arsonists, robbers and murderers, and the king hadn't been able to get rid of them.

"How about this?" the king suggested to the general. "I'll send him on a quest to rid us of the two evil giants. I'll offer him my daughter's hand in marriage and half my kingdom as a dowry if he can kill them, but we both know he will fail. A thousand men couldn't kill those giants, and that will get rid of him once and for all."

"That's brilliant Your Highness," the general said. "I'll

send a hundred horsemen with him as an escort."

When the general told the little man about the king's proposal, he answered, "Of course I'll slay the giants. But I don't need the hundred horsemen. Anyone who can strike down seven with one blow has no reason to be afraid of two giants."

The general swallowed hard. *Maybe the seven he killed weren't men* he thought. *Maybe they were giants!* He had no idea that the little tailor had only killed seven flies!

The next day, the little tailor set out, with the hundred horsemen falling behind. At the edge of the forest he said, "You stay here. I'll take care of the giants myself. I don't want any of you getting hurt!"

As he entered the forest, a cool breeze brought the scent of pine trees. The further he went down the trail, the quieter it became. Soon he heard a loud rumble. As he grew closer, he recognized it as snoring. Two giants were asleep under a tree, snoring so loud and powerfully that the tree limbs rose up and down with their breaths.

The little tailor filled his pockets with stones and climbed high into the tree. He positioned himself so he was over both sleeping giants, and then he started dropping stones on one of them.

At first the giant didn't react, but as the rocks continues to hit him he started swatting them aside. Finally, he sat up and shoved his companion. "Why are you hitting me?" he shouted.

"I'm not hitting you!" the second giant said as he

sleepily rubbed his eyes. "You're having a bad dream."

"Hmmph," the first giant answered, but he lay back down and soon the tree limbs were rising up and down as both the giants resumed their snoring.

The little tailor threw a stone as hard as he could at the second giant. He instantly sat up. "Why are you hitting me?" he yelled at the first giant.

"I'm not hitting you. Leave me alone! I'm sleeping!"

The second giant glared at the first giant, but soon sleep overtook him and he fell back asleep.

Using all his might, the little tailor took his largest stone and threw it as hard as he could aiming at the eye of the second giant. As soon as the stone hit him, the giant sat upright and slammed his fist in the face of the first giant.

The first giant bolted up, grabbed the second giant around the neck and squeezed as hard as he could. The second giant broke free and grabbed a small tree that he used to strike the first giant with all his might. They punched and hit and beat each other until finally both of them lay on the ground unconscious.

The little tailor plunged his sword into their motionless bodies until they were dead.

When he arrived back to the horsemen he said, "Go take the bodies back to the king, boys. The giants are as dead as dead can be, and I'm off to claim my prize."

"But, how did you…What did you do?" sputtered the captain.

Trying to sound modest, the little man said, "Surely you must know that a man like me who can kill seven in a blow isn't troubled by two angry giants. They are beaten and killed by this very sword and they won't trouble anyone ever again." With that, he put the sword into the scabbard and returned to the palace.

The king was startled to learn that the tailor had returned. He didn't really want to give him half his kingdom or his daughter's hand in marriage, and thinking quickly said, "You are such a brave man. I am fortunate that you will soon be my son-in-law, but I must burden you with one more request. In the woods there is a wild unicorn. He attacks anyone who approaches him, and the forest isn't safe. As a favor to your future father-in-law and king, can you please do one more heroic deed and free us from this creature's wrath?"

"Of course, your majesty," the little man replied. "It is the least I can do for my future father-in-law, and because I can kill seven in a blow, I am less afraid of the unicorn than the two giants."

Taking a rope and an ax, he left to find the unicorn. Once again, he told those who followed him to wait behind. The unicorn soon appeared and leaped toward him as if to skewer him with his horn.

"Gently, gently," murmured the tailor. "Not so fast," he encouraged the unicorn. The angry beast paused a moment, and the little man stood still. When the unicorn finally charged him, he waited until the last moment, then he nimbly jumped aside. The unicorn was unable to slow down and thrust its horn into a thick tree.

It pulled and twisted and whinnied and bucked, but no matter what it did the unicorn could not break free. The little man tied a rope around its neck and then cut its horn with his ax. With no horn, the unicorn was as docile as a lamb, and the little man led it back to the castle to present to the king.

The king was beside himself when the little man returned. He didn't want to give away his daughter's hand in marriage or half his kingdom. But he feared the little man who had killed seven in a blow.

He believed this was the most dangerous man in his kingdom, and ordered the wedding to be held promptly with great ceremony, though there was little joy from anyone except the tailor.

A few weeks later, the princess heard the little tailor say in his dreams, "Bring me a patch to fix those trousers," and she realized that the man in her bed was not a great war hero, but a tailor!

She told her father, and the king promised to get rid of her new husband. He told his daughter, "Tonight, leave your bedchamber unlocked. My servants will stand outside, and after he falls asleep, they will go inside and tie him up in ropes and put him on a ship so we will never see him again."

His daughter agreed. Fortunately for the little tailor, the king's squire had taken a liking to him as the tailor had always been kind to him and the other servants. He told the little tailor the king's plan.

That evening, when his wife thought the little tailor was asleep, she unlocked their door and returned to bed. The little tailor, who was only pretending to sleep started shouting, "Bring me a patch to fix those trousers, or I will hit you across your ears with a yardstick. I have struck down seven with one blow, killed two giants and captured a unicorn, so I'm not afraid of anyone who stands just outside my bedroom!"

Hearing his voice, those standing outside the door trembled in fear as they ran away as fast as they could. None of them ever dared to approach him again.

For the rest of his days, all of the people revered him as a brave hero for killing the giants, capturing the unicorn and killing seven in a blow. No one but the little tailor ever knew that the deed he was most famous for was the simple act of killing seven flies.

All of us are on a hero's journey, though many of us seem to have forgotten it. In Greek mythology, those who drank from the river Lethe experienced forgetfulness, and listening to the river's murmuring sound induced drowsiness. Drinking from and listening to the river Lethe made one forget and sleep, but to be a hero we must be awake.

The hero's journey could be described as the effort we must make to be awake. To be awake means that our soul is steering and guiding the direction of our lives. It means our actions are aligned with the desires of our soul, not the anxieties of our mind or ego.

All of us will at times find ourselves in great peril, where the choices we make matter deeply. It is in those moments that an opportunity to be a hero emerges.

One way to identify a heroic choice is that it is often harder than the other options, and it is always the wisest decision. Learning to discern wisdom is a key to heroism.

The story of *The Brave Little Tailor* illustrates that the world's vision of heroism isn't always accurate. While some people the world views as heroes truly exemplify heroism, many praised by the world are no more heroic than the little tailor when he first killed the seven flies.

Ironically, that act, while not heroic on its own, made the tailor *feel* like a hero. It gave him an inner fortitude that allowed him to behave heroically. Like all heroes, he used his strengths. Because he wasn't physically powerful, he found clever ways to prevail.

On the journey to becoming a hero, it is important to recognize that many of our everyday acts are heroic. While the media, society and the world may not praise what we do, our understanding of what is heroic for us should not be external. It must come from within. We need to see the heroic in ourselves.

Many of our most heroic actions are when we subordinate our impulses and desires to what is wise for us. This includes things as simple as finishing an assignment in school when we would rather watch a video, resisting spending money on something we want and paying an urgent bill instead, or saying no to relationships or friendships we know aren't healthy for us.

Heroes act with integrity. When they make mistakes, they promptly admit it and learn from them. Heroes don't tolerate bullying, belittling or abuse in any form. Heroes do the right thing for the right reasons, and they recognize that the ends don't justify the means. They know how they travel on the path they follow is often more important than the destination they reach. They understand that how they comport themselves as heroes is more important than any accomplishment they achieve.

Most heroes are like the little tailor in that some of the things they are recognized for as being heroic, really weren't very heroic at all.

Heroes don't win every battle. Sometimes they are wounded and feel despair. But they get up, learn and try again. The magic in being a hero is that even though they don't win every battle, they always win their wars if they are true to heroic principles.

In its simplest form, being a hero is the practice of doing the right thing, at the right time, for the right reason, even when feeling afraid.

Dragons are a hero's natural companion. It is certain that when we behave heroically, dragons will come to our side and support us.

Chapter Twelve

WALKING WITH DRAGONS

"I know this. Every man gives his life for what he believes. Every woman gives her life for what she believes. Sometimes people believe in little or nothing and so they give their lives to little or nothing. One life is all we have and we live it as we believe in living it and then it's gone. But to surrender who you are and to live without belief is more terrible than dying. Even more terrible than dying young." – Joan of Arc in the play *'Joan of Lorraine'* by Maxwell Anderson

All great heroes have guides. Many of them aren't visible. Some invisible guides, such as our ancestors or deceased parents may seem obvious, others such as angels aren't always apparent. Dragons among the most elusive guides, and rarely do they reveal themselves easily.

Walking with a dragon often means sensing something great and powerful is alongside us, but at most we catch a glimpse out of the corner of our eye, often in a moment we don't expect. Dragons are more likely to appear to us in dreams than waking life, and they are denizens of the internal world of the soul, not the external world of mortality.

If you are afraid that you aren't brave or wise enough for a dragon to help you, stop worrying! Don't be afraid. The birthright of all of us is the ability to walk with dragons. Dragons have been near us since birth. The challenge is to learn to consciously walk with them.

Learning to walk with dragons begins with a commitment to finding our destiny. We have to discover who we really are and learn what is right for us. When we do what is right for us, we gain a sense that our actions, intentions and aspirations are aligning with what we are uniquely here to do.

Once we have a glimpse of who we can become, and an inkling of who we really are, we must reclaim our gift of intuition. We need to trust that we can make wise decisions based on an inner awareness of what is truly right for us.

Our intuition also becomes an internal warning system, so when we are drawn to people, places or things that aren't right for us, we sense or feel that we need to avoid becoming enthralled by whatever is seducing us. Our intuition can act as a lighthouse, warning us away from what would harm or deter us.

All of us struggle with fear. Sometimes the world is overwhelming. Despite that, we need to develop and exercise the muscle of courage. We need the willingness to do the right thing and take action despite our fear.

True courage isn't the absence of fear. It is doing what must be done in spite of fear. It's facing our fear and bravely moving forward despite the paralysis, anxiety and resistance that does its best to derail us.

Life is a series of choices, and meaningful decisions have an opportunity cost. For example, if we choose a boyfriend, girlfriend or spouse, that almost always means we are making a concomitant choice not to choose someone else in that same role. The principle of opportunity cost affects nearly every significant decision we make. Time is limited. Life is short, sometimes much shorter than we think. But regardless of how many years we live, almost every elder will confirm that their time passed quickly and almost every teenager will say that time moves too slowly.

The only way we can balance what is right for us with the near infinite possibilities and choices in life, is to choose wisely. We must develop the ability to discern. Discernment is more than wisdom, analysis, intuition and "gut feeling". It encompasses all these things, but it is collectively greater than any of them.

Discernment requires practice. The more we consciously choose wisely, the more adept we become at practicing discernment. Choices are inevitable. Decisions will always need to be made. Discernment gives us the ability to choose what is right for us. The more we choose wisely the greater our ability to practice discernment.

The foundation of every person who walks with a dragon is their wholeness. This isn't perfection. Life is a journey of development and growth, not arriving at perfection. It is about living a life with a foundation of integrity and "playing with a full deck" or having "all of our parts".

It takes a long time to become a whole person and develop authentic "life-tested" integrity. It begins with not cutting corners, lying and taking advantage of others, but in time it comes from doing the right thing no matter whether anyone is watching. It includes feeling comfortable with our decisions even when we are the only ones who know our motives and actions, especially when we are misjudged. It means doing the right things because they are the right things, even if we think we can get away with doing the wrong things.

Men who walk with dragons can't be immature, nor can they be foolish. There is nothing inherently wrong with immaturity. We all must pass through it, but we can't stay there if we want to walk with dragons.

Wisdom seems to go hand in hand with experience, though not everyone who is experienced is wise. The development of wisdom requires that we examine our lives. We must learn how the consequences of our thoughts, decisions and actions affect our lives and the lives of others. Wisdom is a lifelong practice, but fortunately once we learn to accumulate it, it grows when we nurture it. It is important to water what we want to grow.

No matter how much insight, passion, desire to serve or other motivation we have, if we don't put it into action, it is meaningless. We must actually live our calling in the world.

For most of us, there is a disconnect between our awareness of what we desire to do and who we want to become, and what we actually do on a daily basis. Men who walk with dragons understand that sometimes the greatest battles don't seem so big. They include getting out of bed in the morning and following through with the positive actions planned for this day.

It's easy to make a good plan. It's much harder to start and complete it. To know we have a destiny and then not to do the work to fulfill it is really not to know our destiny at all. While desiring to become who we are destined to be is the beginning of our journey, we must follow that insight with endurance and action.

It is the experience of most of us that distractions, challenges and obstacles will appear between our desire to live our destiny, and the actions we must take to get there. The solution is to persevere no matter what. We must endure to the end. True success is having the courage and discipline to get up one more time than we were knocked down. Fortunately, when we put all we can into living our destiny, dragons and other allies will support us.

Men who walk with dragons understand that the world is sacred. There is great beauty in this world and much here to revere. Looking through some lenses, everything in the world is holy. Men who walk with dragons don't profane the world. They respect it. One of the gifts of respecting the sacred is we grow spiritually and feel a deeper connection to everything around us. Our vision expands and our ability to love and serve grows. In time we realize that none of us are home until all of us are home and how we treat each other is really a reflection of how we feel about ourselves.

All of us are on a quest. What matters isn't so much the outcome. It's our willingness to show up, do the work, and serve others. No matter where we are is perfectly okay as long as our intention is to love and serve, and that is followed up with loving and serving ourselves, that which is greater, and others.

Nothing will draw a dragon to our consciousness quicker than putting everything we have into becoming the person we are intended to be. All of us are holy, one-of-a-kind and wise. We only need to discover and remember it.

When we walk with dragons, we engage with the Mystery. Whatever the transcendent forces that ripple through life that have caught the attention of every society and civilization, our destiny is to embrace, dance, harmonize and allow these forces that our present consciousness can't fully understand to underscore and direct our lives.

It happens for each of us differently as none of us walk

an identical path, though we all travel the road of happy destiny that promises us that if we do our part, Creator or that which is greater will work through us to bring about the highest potential that life can be.

One of our greatest challenges can be a feeling of loneliness. Spiritual growth often feels like a lonely process as it brings into focus the one person we miss most: our highest and best self. The promise of walking with dragons is we will slowly, inexorably, develop a relationship with the person we were destined to meet, and that person is already within us. The love and forgiveness we can learn to feel for ourselves, and the depth of the intimacy we can achieve in bringing together our inner and outer worlds, is one of the most meaningful things any of us will ever do.

Life can be hard. Joy and happiness can be elusive, and we can't always will ourselves into feeling better when we feel lonely, discouraged, depressed and sad. While we can't always make ourselves happy, we can bring meaning to our lives. We bring meaning to our lives through our intentions, actions, persistence and efforts. The most meaningful thing any of us will do is to discover who we really are and then live our calling in this world. It takes a long time, and we generally do it bit by bit, but as long as our mortal body inhabits this earth we can choose to do what is right for us. And doing what is right for us is the truest path to living our destiny and becoming the person we are intended to be.

Some of the signposts that we are on the right path are found in asking ourselves questions like these: Are we kind? Do we love deeply and fully? Do we love the man or woman or child we don't understand? Are we patient with ourselves and others? Do we try to practice wisdom in all our relationships? Are we good stewards of this holy earth? Do we know that we are something more than our thoughts and our bodies and that our essence is eternal? Do we shield secrets from others because we are ashamed, or because we do evil things and don't want to change? Have we integrated all the parts that comprise the essence of who we are and allowed ourselves to grow as a whole person? Have we fully committed to serving that which is greater, rather than serving the anxieties of our mind? Do we love and serve more than we worry and complain?

Walking with dragons is an action. It doesn't come from wishing, imagining or lamenting. Too often we long for what we don't have and mistakenly believe if we were smarter, richer, handsomer or had a different home, car or job that everything would be fine. When we fall into this trap, we have missed the point. We have forgotten that we are the creators, that the dragons were with us all along. The way to get what our heart desires isn't to yearn for what we don't have. It's to be who we really are and recognize that everything worth having is already available to us because we are the creators of the life we live.

The lessons, experience and wisdom in these stories

contain everything one needs to learn to walk with dragons and become the person we are destined to be. Life can be very hard. Sometime it feels so overwhelming that many of us would rather not live anymore, so we think about suicide or we anesthetize ourselves with harmful substances, the internet, loveless sex, gambling, mindless television and anything that will grant respite from the hopelessness we feel.

The promise of taking the adventure of walking with dragons is that our life will have meaning. It doesn't matter if we have given up on life, or are so enthusiastic to grow-up that we can't wait to start our journey!

If we heed the wisdom in these stories, hope, adventure, curiosity and meaning will become part of our everyday lives. While life will still present challenges, we will learn to see them as adventures to experience instead of hopeless circumstances we can't overcome. We learn to love life more than we want to dominate or control it.

There is an old saying that "he who has eyes to see, let him see, and he who has ears to hear, let him hear." What this means is that as we start to use the resources and gifts that allow us to integrate the unseen world with the world we wake up to and survive in, our ability to see and hear things in ways we previously couldn't will grow.

Have you ever listened to something wise that you heard before, but this time it meant something deeper and more profound than when you heard it previously?

As we develop and grow it's as if we are learning a

new language, the language of heart and soul. As we start to walk with dragons we will see and hear things differently. We will see the sacred in the ordinary and the extraordinary in the mundane. We won't be in danger of "climbing a golden staircase to an empty attic," as we will have enough clarity to know where we are, who we serve and what we are here to do. Thoughts of leaving this planet prematurely will leave us, as the urgency of doing all we are destined to do in the little time we are alive here replaces them.

Every one of us is a hero. All of us are special and unique. No matter how many lies society tells us that we may believe, our individual lives matter and all of us are necessary, important, loved and irreplaceable. The greatest lie that keeps us from walking with dragons is "my life doesn't matter."

We live in a culture and society that strips us of hope and meaning and lulls us into a soporific semi-conscious haze with too many unhealthy distractions. Those of us who live in the twenty-first century have more meaningless distractions available to us than any other culture in human history.

The things that matter most can't be purchased in stores or online, nor are they constantly shown on the internet and television.

When we come to the end of this life, what will matter most is how much did we love, who did we serve and how much integrity did we gain. Everything else we sought to acquire, or traded our souls to achieve, will crumble to dust when we take our last breath. So much of what we spend our time pursuing won't matter, so it is wise to start doing what matters most now.

What matter most is to love, serve, explore, learn, teach, grow, make mistakes, learn from them, get betrayed and then heal, love again, serve again, rest, play with little children, watch sunsets, admire the sun and moon, bathe in warm water, enjoy sensuality, love who you are with, be kind to strangers, pray, reflect, play more often with those you love and seek to acquire fewer things and gather more memories. Be brave. Take risks. And always remember that we are never alone, we never were alone, and we will never be alone. I leave you with this blessing given to me by a friend.

"I bless you that you may always have your allies in the earth and stars, that you may always be protected, that you may move easily between worlds, that you may always hear the messages that will guide you, that your light may shine to inspire others, that you may hear the lone voice that needs your help, that you live with your heart and eyes wide open, that you live a life filled with meaning and hope, that you live awake and aware of who you are and who you are intended to be."

My deepest hope is that you always choose to walk with dragons.

AUTHORS NOTE

The stories in *Men Who Walk with Dragons* are interpretations of well-known tales that have stood the test of time. *The Ugly Duckling, The Fir-Tree* and *The Little Match Girl* were written by the great Danish writer Hans Christian Anderson. I cannot definitively ascertain the original author or authors of the other stories. Whoever those unknown storytellers are, they have my deep thanks.

Many thanks to my dear friend Sukey Rosenbaum for her assistance with copyediting. Any remaining mistakes in the manuscript are mine. Thanks to Nancy Schenk for her editorial comments and to Eric Tollefson for his help preparing this book for publication.

www.ingramcontent.com/pod-product-compliance
Lightning Source LLC
Chambersburg PA
CBHW032123170626
46808CB00006B/2080